TEEN FICTION LAS

Laser, Michael.

Cheater

CHEATER

Also by Michael Laser

Dark & Light: A Love Story

6-321

Old Buddy Old Pal

CHEATER

A NOVEL

....

by MICHAEL LASER

DUTTON BOOKS

DUTTON CHILDREN'S BOOKS
A division of Penguin Young Readers Group

PUBLISHED BY THE PENGUIN GROUP

Penguin Group (USA) Inc., 375 Hudson Street, New York, New York 10014, U.S.A. • Penguin Group (Canada), 90 Eglinton Avenue East, Suite 700, Toronto, Ontario, Canada M4P 2Y3 (a division of Pearson Penguin Canada Inc.) • Penguin Books Ltd, 80 Strand, London WC2R 0RL, England • Penguin Ireland, 25 St Stephen's Green, Dublin 2, Ireland (a division of Penguin Books Ltd) • Penguin Group (Australia), 250 Camberwell Road, Camberwell, Victoria 3124, Australia (a division of Pearson Australia Group Pty Ltd) • Penguin Books India Pvt Ltd, 11 Community Centre, Panchsheel Park, New Delhi - 110 017, India • Penguin Group (NZ), 67 Apollo Drive, Rosedale, North Shore 0632, New Zealand (a division of Pearson New Zealand Ltd) • Penguin Books (South Africa) (Pty) Ltd, 24 Sturdee Avenue, Rosebank, Johannesburg 2196, South Africa • Penguin Books Ltd, Registered Offices: 80 Strand, London WC2R 0RL, England

LIBRARY OF CONGRESS CATALOGING-IN-PUBLICATION DATA

Laser, Michael.
Cheater : a novel / by Michael Laser.—1st ed.
p. cm.
Summary: When brilliant high school student Karl Petrofsky gets talked into participating in an elaborate cheating operation at his school, he ends up involved in a bigger problem than he ever anticipated.

ISBN-13: 978-0-525-47826-3
[1. Cheating—Fiction. 2. Peer pressure—Fiction. 3. Conduct of life—Fiction. 4. High schools—Fiction. 5. Schools—Fiction.] I. Title.

PZ7.L32717Ch 2008
[Fic]—dc22   2007018001

Published in the United States by Dutton Books, a division of Penguin Young Readers Group
345 Hudson Street, New York, New York 10014
www.penguin.com/youngreaders

Designed by Jason Henry
Printed in USA • First Edition

10 9 8 7 6 5 4 3 2 1

To my sisters, Anita and Sherry—
for a lifetime of love and support

CHEATER

RULE #1: Don't look up at the teacher to see if the coast is clear. That's like saying, "Is it safe to cheat now?" Instead, cheat coolly, cheat boldly. Focus on the test like a good student should, and use your cheating tools with confidence!!

—A free tip from the Guru

Chapter 1

Call it Petrofsky's Dilemma. Born with the sort of brain that absorbs information the way Bounty paper towels soak up spills, Karl Petrofsky has spent most of his eleven years in school trying to hide the 100s and A+s scrawled across the top of his tests. It's no use, though. Everyone knows, and they all hate him for it—or, okay, that's a bit strong. Let's say they *don't appreciate* how easy school is for him.

Einstein, the jocks call him.

Geek God, shout the skaters, zipping by on their boards.

Intel Inside, quips Mr. Imperiale, handing back Karl's A.P. calculus homework.

Right now, for example, Karl is taking a chemistry test: ionic bonds, covalent bonds, van der Waals forces, that sort of thing. All around him, others sweat and writhe. You can almost hear the gastric juices swishing and bubbling in stressed-out stomachs. Meanwhile, Karl goes down the page, question by question, filling in answers with about as much agitation as a guy taking a survey. (Which of the following is *not* tetrahedral in structure? H_2O. Favorite cookie? Oreo Double Stuf.) It's no wonder that most of his classmates have had the urge, at one time or another, to wring his skinny neck.

This is his biggest problem in life: Unnaturally Powerful Cerebrum → Widespread Social Rejection. Frankly, there have been times when, if a mysterious stranger had offered him Average-Student pills, he would have swallowed the whole bottle. Because he's *not* a nerd, he's not a brownnose, and he hates the identity people have pinned on him. True, he's shy, and trips over his own large feet sometimes, and hasn't yet worked up the nerve to ask a member of the female gender out on a date—but he has friends, and he even makes witty remarks sometimes. Just because he possesses a multigigabyte memory, that doesn't make him a cybertwerp.

(In fact, in his secret fantasy world, Karl likes to imagine himself as a hero—not the muscle-bound type with heavy artillery strapped to his oiled chest, but the subversive kind, the lone skeptic who harpoons pompous fakes with terse, devastating remarks. *That's* the Karl Petrofsky he wishes he could become. Or, if not that, at least not a timid, obedient valedictorian.)

Back in the real world, though—what's a whiz kid to do? He's not desperate enough to intentionally screw up on tests. So far, the only solution he's come up with is to make wisecracks when the opportunity arises, to prove he's not a suck-up—like when Mrs. Olay asked if anyone knew what the Russian czar's son was called, and Karl raised his hand and said, "The Czar-dine?"

In response to which, dead silence fell upon the room.

His friend Lizette got the joke a half hour later, in the hall. "Wait a minute—you meant, like, *sar*-dine?"

"I didn't think it was that subtle."

"Hey, around here, any joke without a toilet in it is subtle."

The periods at Abraham Lincoln High are forty minutes long. Karl finishes the chemistry test in fifteen, but (Petrofsky's Dilemma) he can't hand in his paper, he can't be the first, because that would mean hammering another nail in his own social coffin. Instead, he pretends to check his work, gazing around in between at the rapid tapping of Conor Connolly's right foot, and the visible bra straps under Jasmine Deukmejian's shirt, and the annoyingly upright posture of Phillip Upchurch, who always seems to have a rigid pole up his, ahem.

Blaine Shore glances down at his cell phone, reads the text message there, and calmly goes on with the test. If envy produced a sound—say, the low bubbling of a coffeemaker—then Karl would be loudly gurgling right now. He can't look at Blaine without wishing he could move through life with just a fraction of Mr. Cool's ease and charm. Phillip Upchurch may be every teacher's candidate for ideal student (straight As, infinite community service, and no trace of teen attitude), but Blaine Shore is every student's hero, because he doesn't take anything too seriously, gets pretty good grades without trying, looks a little like a sleepy Brad Pitt, and is a nice guy on top of all that. (The red BMW convertible doesn't hurt the image, either.)

But wait, hold on. What's this? One seat in front of Blaine, Ivan Fretz is peering into the palm of his hand, squinting because he can't make out the tiny words written there in blue ink. Karl remembers Mrs. Kozar scolding Ivan in third grade for his abominable handwriting, and now he sees that she was right: bad penmanship *will* handicap you in all your pursuits.

Ivan peeks around Amy Villarosa's head to make sure Ms. Nudell isn't watching. Oh, what a mistake that turns out to be. The mysterious force that tells us when someone has an eye on us (scientists: please explain this!) tickles Ms. Nudell's sensors, and she glances up from the pile of lab reports she's grading, straight at Ivan. Drawn by teacherly instinct, she floats down the aisle and hovers over him.

He flattens his palm guiltily against the desk.

"Ivan, show me your hand."

"What?" He laughs, looking left and right for support. *What an insane request! This lady must be crazy.*

"Don't waste my time. Just show me the hand."

Though not yet forty, Ms. Nudell has permanent bags under her eyes. Usually, she seems as bored with teaching as her students are bored by her monotonous drone—but when she sees Ivan's crib notes, she comes blazing to life. "Are you serious, Ivan? Am I really seeing this? What are you thinking, that you'll just cheat your way through life and hope nobody notices? This is incredible. Just . . . go. Go away. Get out of my classroom. Take your test, take your hand, and go show them to Mr. Klimchock. Let *him* deal with you. Go! And good luck down there—you'll need it."

Even though Ivan once lied to that same third-grade teacher that Karl stole the M&M's from the mug on her desk (when it was *he* who stole the M&M's, the filthy dog!), and even though Ivan's parents peep over the hedge into Karl's house all the time, Karl can't help feeling sorry for him. Trembling, knocking his chair over, Ivan barely keeps from crying. The humiliation far outweighs the crime.

Once the evildoer is gone, Ms. Nudell decides it's her obligation to deliver the Honesty Lecture. "In case you never gave it any thought before, there really is a purpose in our testing you. That's how we know you're learning, and measure your progress. If you cheat, you don't learn. You defeat the whole purpose of coming here—you waste your time and mine. That's what they mean when they say, 'You're only cheating yourself.'"

Karl appreciates the explanation—really—because the cliché always seemed meaningless before, nonsensical, the opposite of the truth.

While the rest of the class goes back to the business of test taking, Karl daydreams about sending a message via satellite to Ms. Nudell's car radio, *Don't you think you were a bit harsh with the Fretz boy?* And then, right here in this chemistry classroom that smells like vinegar, his life takes a sharp left turn. If you're skimming, you'd better slow down and pay attention.

Just behind Ivan's vacant seat, Blaine is checking his cell phone again. His lips move ever so slightly, as if memorizing the text message. Then he turns his attention to the test paper. Moving his lips again—retrieving the information he needs—he fills in the answer, smiling contentedly.

Blaine Shore is cheating! With his cell phone! After that whole grisly scene!

Unlike Ivan, Mr. Cool doesn't get caught—except by Karl, who gawks with his mouth hanging open.

The same mysterious force that led Ms. Nudell to look up at Ivan now generates a prickling in Blaine's brain. He glances over at Karl, and sees the dumbfounded stare.

Putting one finger to his sealed lips, Blaine gives Karl a wink, checks his phone again, and goes on with the test.

"I never saw Noodle Woman go off like that," says Jonah, in the hall. "She actually looked awake."

"I knew Ivan was slimy," Lizette replies, "but I didn't think he was that dumb. Writing notes on his *hand*?"

"He's dead meat," Matt growls. "Klimchock will eat his brains for lunch. 'One cerebellum sandwich, hold the medulla oblongata.'"

Lizette and Jonah scowl at Matt. Really—the lad does cross the line sometimes.

"Speaking of lunch," Lizette says, "Karl, did you bring us any Jelly Bellies?"

No reply from Karl.

"Paging Karl Petrofsky—are you with us?"

No, he isn't with them. He's still back at his desk, juggling the idea of sleepy-cool Blaine with the text message thing. The two won't stay in his head at the same time.

"Karl, you're scaring us." She bangs her backpack against his arm. "Anybody got a remedy for zombie-bite?"

"What are you talking about?" Karl says, rubbing his arm.

"He's back!"

A voice from a different universe interrupts the banter. "Hey, Karl, can I talk to you for a minute?"

The tall visitor in the striped J. Crew sweater steps between Karl and Lizette.

"I just had a question about the test."

Blaine's straight, white, smiling teeth arouse admiration all by themselves. Karl walks into a water fountain and hits his hip bone, hard.

"Any chance I could get you alone?"

"I'll catch up with you," Karl mumbles to his friends. They head downstairs to the cafeteria, glancing back in perplexity as they go.

Sorry to do this, but if you even think about telling what you saw, I'll send my hired thugs to rip your tongue out.

That's more or less what Karl expects to hear, but Blaine plays it cryptic. "Come on," he says, and leads Karl toward the corner exit, which goes nowhere except to the student parking lot. The strap of Karl's bulging backpack weighs so heavily on his right shoulder that he has to lean leftward to balance it; Blaine, meanwhile, carries nothing at all. He holds out a box of green Tic Tacs, and Karl takes one, not wanting to seem hostile. The Tic Tac turns out to be lime, not wintergreen—an unwelcome surprise, but he can't exactly spit it out and say, *Blechhh,* can he?

There's no one else around. Their footsteps ring and echo on the steel steps.

"I wasn't planning to tell anyone," Karl says.

Blaine throws open the exit door. The bright sun makes both of them blink.

"I didn't think you were, Karl. You're a good guy."

The BMW is parked close to the exit. Blaine unlocks it and gestures for Karl to get in. This may rank as the most confusing moment of Karl's life so far: because, even as he guards against a surprise assault with a lead pipe, he's inflating like a Thanksgiving Day Parade balloon of himself. Blaine Shore considers him a *Good Guy*!

"Where are we going?" he asks.

"It's lunch period. I was thinking about the Leaning Tower."

Before Blaine can climb in, though, someone else flips the driver's seat forward and slips into the back. Karl smells the musky, dusky perfume before he sees her: Cara Nzada, in tight jeans that stop far below her navel and don't seem to have a zipper.

"Hi, Karl."

She knows his name!

The top goes down. Blaine's sunglasses go on. "Everybody good?" he asks.

Karl buckles his shoulder harness. "Mm-hm," he says, feebly.

The wind does a funny thing in a convertible, he discovers. It doesn't hit you in the face, it just makes your hair stand up and dance. In Karl's case, his floppy mop does a high-speed hula.

They drive past his friends, who are blowing up the brown

bags their lunches came in. He hears three loud *pops* in quick succession.

Why does he keep worrying that Blaine is going to drive him to an abandoned warehouse, tie his hands behind his back, and—

"I just wanted to explain why I cheat," Blaine says.

"You don't have to. It doesn't really matter."

"You're wrong. Try to keep an open mind."

"Open up," Cara says, and scratches the top of his head with two fingers.

The spot tingles long after she stops.

"There are two reasons," Blaine begins. "Let's start with the selfish one. You were born with a sticky brain, Karl. You study for half an hour and you know the whole book. Me, I study the same page for three hours and I remember maybe seventy percent. Do I deserve to go to M.I.T.? Absolutely not. I'm not fooling myself. I just want to go to a decent school, get a good job, and enjoy my life. Can you tell me what's wrong with that?"

The way he puts it, it's hard to call his cheating vile. Of course, everything he just said is a rationalizing excuse— but, with Cara's perfume still in his nose, in this car that doesn't have a single crumb on the floor mats or a speck of dust on the dashboard, Karl can't put into words why Blaine is wrong.

"Not exactly," he says.

"Good! Then there's the other reason. You may not have noticed this, Karl, but school is basically unfair. People like you succeed, while other people never do, no matter how hard they try. Teachers make us learn all this information we'll never need, just to sort out the Chosen Few from everybody else."

"You're saying the system doesn't care about us, so it's okay to cheat?"

Blaine examines him uncertainly, between glances at the road. "I can't tell—are you agreeing or disagreeing?"

"Neither, I'm just paraphrasing."

"Oh. Okay." Thrown off, he seems to have lost his place in the script. "Help me out, Cara."

She leans forward. Her smooth black hair glistens. "Karl, what Blaine is saying is total crap."

She rests her hand on Karl's shoulder. Her features are so sharp and delicate, her olive skin so creamy, you could die from the frustrated desire to touch her.

"The reason he cheats, the reason *I* cheat, the reason just about everyone except you cheats—is pure laziness. I can't see studying all night to get the same grade I can get in ten minutes. They like to keep us busy so we won't get into trouble—but I *like* to get into trouble. Why let them steal my life? You won't tell on us, will you?"

She squeezes his shoulder. He meets her cool green eyes.

"Um. No."

"Good man!" Blaine shouts as he pulls into the Leaning Tower's parking lot.

Inside the pizzeria, a mom is feeding her cute, tiny son cut-up mouthfuls of pizza by fork. She gives the three students a friendly smile as they sit down with their slices.

"I knew Karl was all right," Blaine tells Cara as he soaks

the grease from his slice with paper napkins. "I could tell, without ever talking to him."

"*Talk* to him!" the toddler chirps.

Uncomfortable with the flattery, Karl folds his slice and puts the vertex in his mouth.

"So," Blaine says, "would you like to help us?"

In a movie, Karl's first bite of pizza would get caught in his throat, and he would writhe and choke on the floor, looking grotesque and idiotic in front of Blaine and Cara. In the world he really inhabits, though, he only burns the roof of his mouth.

"You okay, Karl?"

"Good pizza, huh?" says Cara, amused.

He breathes in and out through O-shaped lips, delivering cool air to his palate while waiting for them to say, *Had you scared there for a minute, didn't we?*

"We've wanted to ask you for a long time. I just didn't want to take a chance on you turning us in. But, now that you know . . . how about it?"

Over the cash register, the cartoon tower of pizza leans humorously to the left. An anchovy hangs on to the edge, trying not to fall off. How long can Karl go without answering Blaine's question? Let's see—twenty seconds. Thirty seconds.

Forty seconds. Fifty.

"What do you think, Karl?" Blaine prods.

"WHAT ARE YOU TALKING ABOUT?"

"I know what's going on in your mind," Blaine says. "You're thinking, *Why should I help them? What's in it for me?*"

"That's not what I was thinking."

"It's a valid question. Why in the world would you help us cheat, when you yourself don't need help—when you would only be helping others?"

"I'll tell you one reason, Karl," Cara says. She sips through her straw. "We would both be extremely grateful."

"And so would a lot of other people. Everyone would stop thinking you're just a geek, a brain on two feet who only looks out for Number One. They would see the good guy behind the goofy exterior. A generous person, willing to help the rest of us poor slobs."

"You would be unique," Cara says. "The Genius Who Cares."

Her lips are thin, her smile crooked and sort of mocking, as if all of this is just teasing and only a fool would take it seriously. On the other hand, she keeps gazing into his eyes like a snake charmer.

Behind the counter, the pizza guys are watching a soccer game with the commentary in Spanish. The cute kid pounds the table and studies his fist curiously. Ordinary though his surroundings may seem, Karl has the feeling he has fallen down a rabbit hole. Tumbling dizzily, end over end, he hears people say things they would never say in real life—Blaine inviting him cheerfully to cheat, Cara Nzada almost flirting with him. Any minute now, men made of playing cards may start swinging axes at his neck.

"I'll tell you what I like about you, Karl," Cara says. "You don't pretend to be cooler than you are. You're just *you*. That's a good thing—but you need to break out of your little world. Don't be so afraid! You have the potential to be more than a brilliant nerd and a social disaster."

Obviously, she's manipulating him—shamelessly, outrageously. If he could make a wish, though, it would be for her to keep going.

She reaches over and puts her hand on top of his. It's cold from the soda can. "Is your life so wonderful the way it is that you don't want it to ever change?"

He sits very still and waits for these hallucinations to end.

"It's kind of fun to break the rules," she says.

She strokes the backs of his fingers with one of hers, and he looks up again. In her eyes, he sees the strangest sight of all: a small person flying through the air.

"Bye bye bye!" the little boy calls happily as his mother carries him, over her head, out of the pizzeria.

Karl, too, is flying. If only he could get back to solid ground.

RULE #2: The stakes are high, so think twice
before you brag to a buddy who may blab your
secrets around the school--because, if your bud
blabs to the wrong person, you're going down
like the Titanic.

Chapter 2

Okay. *What do you want me to do?*

Are these the words you're expecting poor bedazzled Karl to mumble? Don't hold your breath. Even in the face of Cara's flirtation and Blaine's confusing logic—even though part of him longs to keep sitting here with this gorgeous pair, as if they were all friends—Karl is still Karl, and he has more common sense than your stereotypical math genius or absentminded professor.

"So, are you with us?" Blaine asks optimistically.

"Are you crazy?" Karl sputters. "*NO*, I'm not with you!"

The only question in his mind, really, is whether or not to walk straight out the door. He chooses not to, mostly because it would seem hostile, but also because he would have to jog the mile and a half back to school.

Blaine takes the rejection amiably. "You never know unless you ask."

Cara gives Karl a mischievous grin. "I hope you don't look down on us, Karl—just because we weren't born with your advantages."

"I'm not looking down on you."

"That's good. Because, if you change your mind, the door's always open."

An awkward patch follows. Karl watches the Ecuadorian team score a goal on the TV, and is grateful to the announcer for filling the silence with his crazed howl, "GOOOOOOOOOOOOAL!"

At the last minute, Blaine and Cara decide to skip the last three periods, leaving Karl in a minor panic—even at a sprint, he'll get to German late—but Blaine generously offers to drop him off a block from school. His last words, as Karl climbs out of the car: "Don't worry, amigo. Be happy."

Cara's hair whips behind her as she waves good-bye, arm straight up, looking forward, not back.

Of all the mind-bending words spoken that lunch period, these are the ones that haunt Karl: *Is your life so wonderful the way it is that you don't want it to ever change?*

His friends are coming out of the cafeteria with aluminum foil antennae sticking up out of their hair (or, in Lizette's case, her baseball cap). So soon after gazing into Cara's green eyes, the three of them are not a pretty sight. Jonah has enough steel on his gigantic teeth to open a small hardware store, and his hair stands up like stiff straw. Tiny Matt can't keep all of his body parts still at the same time. (No, it's not a neurological disorder, just a case of hyperactivity he should have outgrown by now.) And Lizette—well, actually, Karl found her so appealing when she first moved here from Florida that he almost got up the nerve to ask her for a date (she's a tall beanpole just like him, with shaggy, short-ish, chestnut hair, a long nose, and a southern accent, and the whole package just tugged at his heart, in part because she seemed to actually *like* him), but Jonah fortunately pointed out that she was obviously gay before Karl embarrassed himself. With her Devil Rays cap pulled down to her eyebrows and her loose gray sweat suit, she could easily pass for a guy—to be honest, her nonhetero orientation is what took the pressure off and let him relax around her and become friends—but right now, Karl wishes she would dress just a little more attractively, no matter which gender she prefers.

Yes, he knows it's disloyal, superficial, and basically odious to judge his friends by their exteriors, but the radiance of Blaine and Cara has blinded him temporarily, and he's still waiting for his eyes to adjust.

"Where'd you disappear to?" Jonah asks. "What did Sweater Boy want with you?"

"We saw you drive away with him," Lizette says accusingly. "Very strange, Karl."

"He just wanted me to explain something. From the chem test."

"Like what?" Matt demands, arched eyebrows leaping, as if to say, *Now we've got you.* "Ionic bonds? Savings bonds? Barry Bonds?"

The school bell sounds—not a bell, really, but the five-note beginning of reveille, played on tinkly chimes. Karl never noticed before how obnoxious this recording is.

"Hydrogen bonding," he mumbles. "He just wanted to know—"

"Okay, okay," Lizette says, "stop, we surrender. Turn off your Lethal Boredom Ray."

After school, he whips through his calculus, history, and music theory homework so he can get to work in the garage. Karl's parents have always worked long hours, and from toddlerhood on, he has learned to entertain himself with projects of his own devising. In fourth grade, he built a Hamster Generator, which enabled little Hamilton to power his own night-light by running on his wheel. In ninth grade, he concocted a thermosensitive paint, which turned silvery gray in the heat and black in the cold; his parents let him coat the shingles with it, and now the roof absorbs the sun's warmth in winter and bounces it away in summer. (Unfortunately, the U.S. Patent Office wrote back that Armine Fodek of Chillicothe, Ohio, had a similar patent pending.) At present he's working on his most ambitious project to date—but he refuses to tell a soul what it is until he finishes and tests it. Suffice it to say that this project blends elements of fluid mechanics, combustion, and sound, and that working on it absorbs him completely.

While tinkering in the garage with an ignition device, adjusting the flame size, he hears a loud motorcycle engine and looks outside. It's his neighbor Norbert, the apprentice electrician, coming out of his parents' garage. A girl holds on to his waist from behind, orange hair flying out from beneath her helmet as they roar away.

When the noise fades away, he looks at the pipe wrench in his hand and hears Cara again: *Is your life so wonderful the way it is?*

His father stops in the garage on his way inside. Karl quickly blows out the flame and covers it with the small, galvanized pail he keeps at hand for this purpose, then pulls the paint-stained Goofy and Pluto sheet over the workbench.

"I just hope," Dad says, "that whatever it is can't be hijacked by enemy combatants and used to wreak havoc on our streets."

"No comment."

(At least Dad is semifunny, unlike Ivan Fretz, who threw out a mocking guess last week while walking the family Labradoodle: "A robot girlfriend?")

Over a late dinner, Karl's parents cheerily discuss the family's college touring schedule: Princeton and Penn one week; Yale to Brown to Harvard the next, with a possible stop at M.I.T.; and Columbia the first afternoon they can both take off work. The issue of Stanford inspires some teasing. "You wouldn't really want to put that many miles between us, would you?" his dad asks.

Karl thinks it over. His feelings are mixed.

"I don't know," he says. "What's it worth to you to keep me on the East Coast?"

His mom cuts the joking short. "You need to prepare some questions in advance. How accessible the professors are, class sizes, how happy the students are in general. And you should decide if you want to sit in on a class at each school."

"It'll be good to spend some time together," his father says. "For once in our hectic lives."

Karl sort of agrees, but he also wonders how it'll be, spending several entire days traveling around with his parents. Part of him already wants to scream, *Let me out! I'll do anything! Just get me out of this car!*

Since he can't share that with them, he raises a different issue. "I don't think those schools are going to take me. All I have is grades."

His father hunches closer to the center of the table, as if spies from a competing family might be listening in. "I talked to a private college adviser," he confides. "According to her, some universities would consider your independent work an acceptable substitute for standard extracurricular activities. If it's impressive enough."

"*What* independent work?" Karl practically spits.

"Your Mystery Project. What else?"

Just as he feared.

"You'll finish before it's time to apply, right? You've got"— he counts on his fingers—"seven months."

"Sure, I'll finish, but—that's not—that's—personal. I'm not doing it to impress a college."

"Perfect!" his mother says, and squeezes his hand. "You're driven by your own passionate curiosity, not by a desire for self-advancement. If they're impressed, that's just . . ."

"Incidental," his father offers.

"Gravy."

"The icing on the cake."

Could they be happier with their brilliant son? Not much. In their different ways, they have both placed all of their hopeful ambition squarely on Karl's shoulders. His father, a tax lawyer, went to a state college near the Canadian border and has always felt dwarfed, status-wise, by his Ivy League partners. His mother, right-hand woman to Manhattan real estate developer Paul Tralikian, has an M.B.A. from Wharton but considers herself the dimmest light among her siblings, a neurosurgeon, a judge, and a congresswoman. By a happy accident of fate and biology, Karl's brain turned out to be a more powerful engine than either of theirs, and they have reason to believe (ecstatically) that he will achieve more than either of them ever hoped to.

And he knows it.

Is your life so wonderful the way it is . . .

Lying in bed in the dark, he analyzes the situation this way:

His parents want him, always, to stay ahead of the pack. But *ahead of the pack* means all by himself, out there in front of everybody else, looking over his shoulder at people who resent him for being so far beyond them. Is it right to strive to do better than everyone else? Isn't it a little . . . greedy? Truth is, the whole Number One Student thing disgusts him. Much more appealing than any superachiever are the graceful, confident, beautiful ones—people like Cara and Blaine.

He remembers her hand on his—cool, and so soft—and her amazing green eyes, and the thin-lipped, mocking smile. The fact that it was pure manipulation doesn't stop him from wanting more.

Usually, he falls asleep within ninety seconds of lying down. Not tonight, though. Not even close.

But each new day is a fresh start, and even with crusty gunk cementing his eyes shut, Karl accepts the sunshine on his face and gladly observes his spirit rising from the muck of yesterday. No, his life isn't perfect—but what does that have to do with cheating? Not a thing.

Even the dull routine of school feels comforting today. Yes, it's a strange and absurd place—with pepless pep rallies, longer hours spent preparing for standardized tests than on any actual subject, teachers who act like exhausted bureaucrats waiting to collect their pensions, and a principal who hasn't been seen in months (rumor has it he suffered a nervous breakdown long ago and the assistant principal has him locked away in an attic storeroom)—but, viewed with the right distance, the absurdities can be seen as amusing.

For example: the assistant principal calls an assembly during seventh period. Recent assemblies have featured a rotund dietician who lectured them on the perils of junk food, and a uniformed police officer who tried to instill in them a righteous terror of scooters, skateboards, and Rollerblades. ("Gore and mayhem on wheels," in his words.) You never know what kind of preposterous harangue you're in for at one of Mr. Klimchock's assemblies.

"He's going to announce a new dress code," Jonah predicts. "Shorts in the winter and plastic sweat suits in the summer."

Lizette shakes her head. "I say he'll make room for more test prep by cutting out chemistry and history."

Though too sleepy to contribute, Karl enjoys listening to their quips. That is, until Klimchock opens his mouth.

"Cheating," the assistant principal says, breathing into the microphone, deep as death.

Mostly hidden behind the lectern, Klimchock lets them wait for the rest of the sentence. The steel rims of his glasses catch the spotlights and concentrate them in two painfully bright specks; a larger patch of light shines on his polished pink scalp.

"Cheating," he repeats, this time in his usual sonorous baritone. "Is. Epidemic."

The oddly disconnected delivery catches the students' attention but also makes some of them wonder if he has gone insane.

Mr. Klimchock, a small, sturdy man, gives the impression of great density, as if a football player had been compressed to the size of a jockey. His mouth curls sourly as he informs the students, "You may not think we know what you're doing. But. We. Do."

Careful not to turn his head, Karl swivels his eyeballs all the way to the right, far enough to see Ivan at the end of the row. Ivan seems to have suffered an attack of premature rigor mortis.

"In order to stop you, we're going to have to get tough. You leave us no alternative. If your generation understood the meaning of honor, things would be different, but the word seems to have fallen out of use. Can anyone here define it? Can you, Mr. Fretz?"

Corpses can't speak, and neither can Ivan.

"I thought not. And so, we fall back on the old methods. Reward and punishment, the carrot and the stick. Each has its adherents. Which way do you think I lean? Mr. Fretz? Care to guess?"

Eyeballs straining painfully sideways, Karl detects movement on Ivan's face: his lower lip is trembling.

"Rhetorical question, no need to answer. So, let's get down to business. You cheat, because honor means nothing to you. All right. Now you're caught. (Isn't it sad? After all these years in school, you still haven't learned that *we can see you* from the front of the room.) You cheat. You're caught. What shall we do with you? What do they do at other schools? I'll tell you some of the options." Here Mr. Klimchock, in his sober brown suit, raises his pitch to a namby-pamby drone. "'First offense, zero on the test. Second offense, course grade lowered. Third offense, fail the class, detention, community service, notify parents.' What horse manure! Cut to the chase! Throw the criminals out and be done with it!"

The trembling has spread to Ivan's entire head.

"As it happens, I'm not the expelling kind. I've got a different plan. Are you ready? *If you cheat and get caught, a note will be attached to both your student record and your official transcript.* You will NOT have the opportunity to expunge it. Every college you apply to will see this note. We're pioneers here, in the war against cheating. Some would call the penalty harsh, but I say it's only fair. Agreement? Disagreement?"

Silence has fallen on the auditorium—absolute, except for the faint buzz of the microphone.

"What will the admissions officer think when he sees

a note, in bold type, saying, **Ivan Fretz cheated during a Chemistry exam**? Consider that the college has two thousand applications for five hundred slots, and this admissions officer is tired, very tired, his eyes are twitching from overwork. Well, you never know. He may be a generous, forgiving soul. Then again, let's get real."

The air in the auditorium has thickened to a paste of astonished horror. Even by the standards of Abraham Lincoln High, this speech strikes the students as outrageous, demented. Klimchock, it seems, has flipped his beany.

An anonymous student calls out, "April Fool," although that was two days ago.

Mr. Klimchock doesn't hunt down the offender, or even acknowledge the outburst.

"Please stand up, Mr. Fretz."

Ivan stands, though not to his full height. He stays slightly bent, cowering—and that sight flips a switch in Karl's brain. Not that Ivan is an admirable or even likable person, but old memories are seeping back, from the prekindergarten days when Karl used to go over to Ivan's house to play, and his messy mom would serve them chocolate chip cookies at a jelly-smeared kitchen table already covered with crumbs, and one time Karl refused to interrupt a game of Candy Land to go pee and then it was too late and he wet his underwear and Mrs. Fretz lent him a clean pair of Ivan's Batman briefs, and washed and dried Karl's underwear before he went home, saying, "I won't tell if you won't tell."

"You will serve as an example to the rest of the school, Mr. Fretz. You will have a note attached to both your record and your transcript. The next student caught cheating will have the same and will also be suspended. Welcome to the new zero tolerance policy. And, because I believe in positive reinforcement as well, anyone who reports a cheater will receive the Lincoln High School Honor Code Award— which, I admit, is just a certificate that I haven't designed yet, but the words will look quite impressive on a college application."

Ivan's head has been dropping slowly, steadily. His upper body is now nearly horizontal, as if he were bowing to the assistant principal.

Karl wishes he could give Ivan the strength to stand tall, to walk out of the auditorium, place himself between the pillars at the front door and, like Samson, push them apart until the whole building collapses.

But no one can give Ivan that strength, and anyway, the pillars are too far apart. If this cruel school is to come tumbling down, someone will have to find a different way.

The tiles in the bathroom are supposed to evoke the blue Caribbean, but to Karl, they look more like the chlorine stain in his grandmother's bathtub.

While he's washing his hands, Blaine Shore appears behind him like a conscience angel. "Quite a guy, that Klimchock. He forgot to say, 'Mwa-ah-ah.'"

Karl's hands are shaking. He watches them as if they belonged to someone else.

Blaine wanders over to the stalls and taps his fingernails against the putty-colored steel, where a graffitist has written ASSISTANT PRINCIPAL'S OFFICE—DO NOT DISTURB. "I just had to ask," he says. "I know you said you wouldn't mention what you saw, but I just wanted to make sure, since—"

"I'll help you," Karl croaks.

Blaine doesn't answer right away. Caught by surprise, he half-smiles but doesn't seem to understand what sort of help Karl is offering. "You will?"

"You wanted me to cheat with you and Cara. I changed my mind. I'll do it."

The half-smile opens up into the real thing. "Sweet," he says and puts a friendly hand on Karl's shoulder.

Blaine's features fit his face perfectly, in both size and placement. By contrast, Karl's eyes are a bit too close together, and his jaw is too narrow. His reflection in the bathroom mirror would depress him, except for Blaine's enthusiastic gratitude. With a new friend like this, there's no telling how his life may change.

Yeah, his inner pessimist comments. *Maybe you'll end up in jail.*

Chapter 3

Where can a bunch of teenagers conspire to overthrow the established order without attracting attention?

Duh.

In the middle of the food court at Eden Tree Mall, at a rectangular table formed by pushing together two small square ones, Blaine introduces Karl with a sweep of the arm. "Meet the Confederacy, Karl."

The soldiers in this rogue army are:

Vijay Roy, crisply attired in white shirt and dark slacks.

Tim Bean, mischievous prankster slob, whose stringy dreadlocks have earned him the nickname Rasta Pasta Man.

Ian Higgins, bored as always, tapping his nose pensively with a plastic spork.

And Noah Marcus, foamer at the mouth, whose T-shirt of the day reads DISMANTLE THE MACHINE. (ASK ME HOW.)

Karl has known these people for years, though not well. That they have teamed up with Blaine and Cara to outwit their teachers and cheat their way through high school boggles his mind. The student body at Abraham Lincoln divides fairly neatly into subcultures—Preps, Goths, Skaters, Druggies, Jock Brutes, Politicos, Science Nerds, and Outcasts— and Karl would have placed each of the cheaters in a different one of these slots (Vijay has been programming computers since he got out of diapers, Tim giggles inexplicably at random moments, Ian wears khaki twenty-four hours a day, and Noah owns so many ideological T-shirts that Karl has never seen the same one twice), but they've all fooled him. Like undercover CIA agents, they have used their various styles as camouflage for their true identities.

The seven blue trays don't quite fit on the two small tables, so the first moments of Karl's membership in the Confederacy are taken up with rearranging the chicken strips, Beef-Ka-Bob, meatball marinara sub, egg drop soup, Double-Decker Taco Supreme, and Mango Smoothie.

Is it his imagination, or is there an unfriendly tension in the air? None of them, except Blaine and Cara, will look him in the eye, and there isn't a heck of a lot of chitchat, either.

"Karl, are you a spy for Klimchock?" Blaine asks casually.

He doesn't get the point. "Uh. No."

"I'm convinced," Ian says, meaning the opposite.

Now Karl understands the averted gazes. They're like Mafiosi hiding their faces behind newspapers as they climb the courthouse steps.

"Are you kidding?" Karl begins. "You think—"

Cara cuts him off. "You people don't understand Karl.

You're such feeble judges of character! Just because he's smart, that doesn't mean he's on the other side. Karl has a deep inner longing to defy authority and prove he's more than a brain. Am I right, Karl?"

That she understands him so well—that she has *noticed him*—makes Karl's heart flutter. It's one of the great moments in his life so far, right up there with winning the backstroke race at Camp Wakanaki.

"You're right," he says.

"Let's stop wasting time," Blaine tells his band of cheaters, "and show our new comrade what's what."

While the P.A. system thumps a song no one can identify over the many voices and clattering trays, and Tim hums the *Mission: Impossible* theme, Vijay reveals the secret tools of the Confederacy: (1) the graphing calculator programmed so that a swift series of keystrokes brings up handy formulas, such as: A'S ATOMIC NUMBER x A'S ION CHARGE = B'S ATOMIC NUMBER x B'S ION CHARGE; (2) the CD Walkman that plays not 50 Cent, as the disk's label advertises, but Vijay's voice reciting key dates and events leading up to the Civil War; (3) the small wireless camera taped to his wrist under his shirt cuff, which transmits the fine print on Noah's Giant Roast Beef sandwich wrapper to Cara's laptop monitor (the blue letters on the crinkled foil are clearly legible, as is the cowboy hat logo); and (4) the iPod loaded with songs whose titles, conveniently, are French vocabulary words with their English translations.

"Technology," Tim intones. "Better tools for better living."

"Don't forget my cell phone," Blaine adds. "Before the chemistry test, I sent myself a few helpful text messages."

"Personally, I don't completely trust computers," Cara says. "They tend to crash right when you need them most. I like to back myself up with a hard copy."

She flips up the hem of her short skirt to reveal typed notes taped to the inside.

"She's just an old-fashioned girl," Vijay says.

"The best part is, they can't demand to see my notes."

Though there's some nausea mingled with his amazement, Karl covers that up and asks, "Do you guys buy term papers online?"

"Not anymore," replies Blaine. "The teachers have a search service that scans for plagiarism. That's one of the reasons why we want your help."

Wouldn't it be easier, Karl wonders, *to just study?*

Uncharacteristically bold, he asks the question out loud.

Mount Noah erupts. "Skipping the work isn't the point!" (Cara gives Karl a flicker of a smile, *Just humor him*.) "School is a machine serving a warped society. Its purpose isn't to teach, it's to sort us out—who gets to go to Harvard and who gets to clean toilets. If it was really about learning, grades wouldn't matter. The Machine doesn't care about us. Why should we care about the Machine? Sabotage it! Rebel! Cheating is freedom! Cheating is integrity!"

A bit of Noah's cinnamon bun comes flying out and lands on Karl's plate. "Is that what the rest of you think?" he asks.

"I think he needs medication," Tim says.

"Then why do you cheat?"

"Uhhhh—for fun?"

"School is so tedious otherwise," Ian says.

"Everyone is doing it," Blaine adds. "If I don't, I'm at a disadvantage."

Cara comments, "This is how America works, Karl. People cheat whenever they can—on taxes, on the golf course, in elections. You know who lives by Boy Scout ethics? Nobody."

"You're putting me to sleep," Ian complains. Making his own fun, he flings a nugget of sesame chicken over his shoulder. The breaded missile lands on a blind lady's table; her dog leaps to its feet, claws scratching the stone tile floor.

"To me, it's a sport, a technical challenge," Vijay explains. "We invent a system—they catch on—we refine the system. Mr. Imperiale makes everyone erase the memory in our calculators—so I program mine to *look* like the memory's erased, but really everything's still there, in cache."

"I hope you're impressed, Karl," says Cara. "I know I am."

He doesn't know what to say. He's not sure what he thinks or which way is up.

"There's one other thing to teach you," Blaine says. "The Code."

"You mean for communicating in secret?"

"No, Code as in Code of Behavior. What is The Code, rebels?"

"Do not share our methods with outsiders," Noah warns, pointing at Karl, Uncle Sam style. "One of our former members did that, and he got caught the next day. Coincidence? I think not."

"Even if they see you cheat, deny everything," Tim says, smirking.

"And most important of all"—a steely gaze from Blaine—
"if you get caught, you go down alone. Never reveal the
names of your comrades."

A hunk of meatball has gotten stuck halfway down Karl's
throat, or at least it feels that way: a large, distressing
mass, close to his heart, that doesn't belong there. He
focuses on his plate, wishing he could make the world go
back to normal.

"Come take a walk with me, Karl."

Cara puts her hand on his—that softness again!—and
keeps it there until he stands. She leads the way out of the
food court, over to the square fountain where the spokes of
the mall converge.

Small children lean on the low marble ledge and harass
their mothers for pennies. "I want a wish!" one girl insists.
Cara sits down on the ledge, and Karl sits near her.

"Second thoughts?"

She has on a fuzzy white short-sleeved sweater with a
low, scooped neck. The fuzz blurs her edges.

"I'm just—uncomfortable."

"Makes sense to me. Getting used to a new universe
takes time."

She's doing it again, melting his brain. You don't expect
someone who looks like Cara and dresses like Cara to see
into your soul.

"So, what do you think, are you going to back out? Please
say no."

"I can't, right? Now that I know their secrets—they'd
hunt me down like a dog."

Her laugh is a squawk. Doesn't matter: the fuzz is soft enough to make up for it.

A kid with long tangled hair hurls a penny sideways, and it hits Karl's cheek. "Sorry!" the mom calls over. Cara takes the penny from Karl's thigh and holds it out to the little munchkin. "You're pretty," she says, as the tiny fingers grab the penny.

"I'm a boy!" the kid protests.

They lock their laughter inside. If she were a different person, then someday they might end up in front of a fireplace together, reminiscing. *Remember the kid at the fountain? That was so funny!*

"I have a philosophical question for you, Karl. Is a code of honor worth anything if you're the only one in the world who lives by it? Isn't that more like a crazy personal obsession?"

"I'm not sure. You've got me pretty confused."

At a nearby kiosk, a green river flows beneath the Brooklyn Bridge, one of many lit-from-behind pictures for sale. The water looks so real—but it isn't.

"Well, Karl? Are you in or out?"

He can't answer, isn't sure, just sits there like a stunned fool. She slides across the hard marble until her knee touches his. The fuzz on her sweater shifts, too, drawn toward him by static electricity. "I wonder what I'd see if I could peek into your brain," she says.

The truth? She'd only see perplexity. He can't understand why she's flirting like this, when she can't possibly want anything from him except the right answers.

A little splash hits their hands.

"You should toss a penny," she says. "Make a wish. You never know."

The water that falls from the square central pool into the surrounding well makes a soothing *sssssshhhhhhh*—but it's not soothing enough to keep his face from reddening.

"No. I don't think so."

"Karl—all the brains in the world won't do you much good if you think you're beat before you start."

He sits silently, his insides gnarled, and waits for the turmoil to end.

She rubs her arm up against his. "Courage, Karl. Your world is about to change for the way better."

She tousles his hair and heads back to the food court. Karl stays on the ledge a while longer, watching the long rippling sheet of water spill into the well. Little waves cross the narrow channel and then bounce back again, making the bright copper pennies below seem to shift back and forth. Now they're here, now they're there—but where are they really?

Something strikes his arm. A second later—it takes that long to process the information—pain shoots up and down, to his elbow and his shoulder.

"What did I just see?"

Lizette is holding a softball bat, tightly wrapped in a Sports Authority bag.

"Are you out of your mind? You hit me with a bat!"

"It was a checked swing. And don't change the subject. What's happening here, Karl?"

Sneaky and guilty, he steals a glance at the food court. Cara reports to the others, shaking her head.

"Why would Cara Nzada rub her arm on you? Something real strange is going on."

"No it's not. She just . . ."

But the famed Petrofsky Cerebrum comes up blank. (What if Lizette asks how he got here, when he doesn't have his license yet? What will he say?)

"I know what it's about, Karl. Your face gives it all away."

His mouth, he realizes, is hanging open. He shuts it before small insects can fly in.

"There's only one thing a girl like that wants from a guy like you."

Lost, he waits for clarification.

"She wants to copy your homework, right?"

"Yes!" he lies, happily.

"It's not a good thing, Karl."

"I know."

A boy is pointing at the Brooklyn Bridge picture, tugging on his mother's arm, begging her to buy it. The mom has her doubts.

"So what did you tell her?"

Karl keeps quiet.

"Don't tell me you said okay!"

"I said maybe."

She shakes her head, upset for real now, no longer teasing—if she ever was. "All she had to do was rub your arm."

For an instant, he feels the unfairness of this world, where girls like Cara get treated like royalty and girls like Lizette get ignored, at best.

Wait. Is Lizette *jealous*?

But that would only make sense if she . . .

Behind Lizette, Blaine is waving to Karl. The Confederacy is leaving, threading its way out of the food court, toward the exit doors. Cara blows him a kiss.

Lizette turns to see what he's looking at. Fortunately, Cara has passed behind the Piercing Pagoda.

"Seems like we're dealing with a case of A.D.D. today."

"Hm?"

She grabs her baseball cap and raises it into whacking position, but gives up. "You're gonna wear out my hittin' arm."

In the fountain, the waters lap quietly. The many coins shift back and forth, back and forth, an illusion that makes Karl a bit seasick. He can't remember lying to Lizette before today, and he would really like to never do it again.

"How'd you get here, anyway?" she asks. "You take the bus?"

"Uh-huh," he lies.

"Well, if you promise not to do anything perverted, I'll give you a ride home. What'd you come here to shop for, anyway?"

"I don't know—just looking around."

She shakes her head. "Seems like there's a lot you don't know."

Understatement of the year, he thinks.

RULE #4: It's not how excellent your cheating methods are—it's how excellently you execute them. Think of it like golf. If you want to be Tiger Woods, you have to practice, practice, practice!

Chapter 4

COMMANDO KARL'S ROOKIE MISSION

TARGET: *German quiz—prepositions*

RECEIVERS: *Tim, Ian*

APPARATUS: *spy mike, earphones*

DEFENSIVE BARRIER: *Herr Franklin*

RISK OF DETECTION: *low*

No room for second thoughts, attacks of conscience, or chickening out now. Tyranny must be opposed, as Blaine reminded him. The cruel Klimchock must be defeated, one test at a time.

The wireless mike sewn inside his collar, behind the top button, weighs next to nothing. Tim and Ian have their earphones in—not the usual white buds, but imperceptible flesh-tone itty-bitties. The members of the Confederacy give him last-minute encouragements as he makes his way down the hall: a pat on the back, an arm squeeze. "Concentration," Vijay whispers. "Just relax," Blaine says.

I should have practiced more, Karl thinks.

Tim stops in his tracks as they enter. "Oh no. He installed a Zorbo-Scope!"

Karl searches the room, panicking, for the half second before he realizes it's a joke.

"Steady there, soldier," Ian says.

At his desk, he takes three deep breaths.

"You okay?"

That's Jonah, to his right. A ghost from his previous, law-abiding life.

"Yeah, why?"

"You look like you might throw up."

"*Willkommen,*" says Herr Franklin—better known to his students as Doctor Franklinstein. He counts quiz sheets and hands them to the first student in each row. "Please keep them facedown until I tell you. You're on your honor."

The quiz sheets run out before Karl gets one. He has to raise his hand. Herr Franklin comes briskly, apologetically, special delivery. Flakes of dandruff rain down on the desk.

"All right. Now this is stuff we've gone over and over, so I'm expecting every one of you to ace it. Don't disappoint me."

"We won't," says Tim.

"That's the attitude I like to see. Is everybody ready? *Nehmt euere Bleistifte raus. Eins, zwei, drei, und . . . fangt mal an!*"

The quiz is so easy, it seems a waste to cheat—but Karl understands, this is a trial run, meant to build his confidence. *Fill in the missing prepositions that take the dative case: aus, ___, bei, ___, nach, ___, von, ___.* Same for accusative case, and for the doubtful prepositions, which Herr F. likes to call the switch-hitters.

When the teacher returns to his desk up front, Karl leans in close to the desk, concealing his face behind Justin Pflamm's back. "Dative," he whispers into his collar, moving his lips as little as possible. *"Ausser . . . mit . . . seit . . . zu."*

Something hits him on the left side of the head. There it is, down on the floor by his sneaker: a tiny red and black eraser in the shape of a ladybug. Ian is jabbing his own collar with his finger, mouthing the words, *Turn the mike on!*

Oops.

After sliding the switch from twelve o'clock to four, Karl repeats the message. Ian gives him a discreet thumbs-up.

"Five more minutes," Herr F. announces and goes to his supply closet in the back of the room. A stack of canary yellow paper spills from the top shelf, all over the floor. "Dingus!" blurts Herr F., squatting to clean up the bright mess. "Never mind. Just concentrate on your work."

Karl obeys. He's on the very last preposition, *zwischen*, when Herr F., alongside him, says, "Pardon?"

What does a heart really do at moments like this: stop or sink? Neither, to be physiologically accurate. It would be entirely correct, however, to say *the blood deserts Karl's face like helpless villagers fleeing a volcanic eruption.*

"Did you say something, Karl?" Herr F. asks.

"I must have been thinking out loud."

"That's a bad habit during tests." The teacher laughs. "Better keep those answers to yourself!"

Chuckle, chuckle. Not for a moment, though, is Karl in danger of getting caught.

Passing his quiz forward—mission accomplished—Karl glances at Ian, who sends him a congenial nod.

The Confederacy meets at lunchtime at Blaine's car, where high fives and yee-has are awarded to the rookie cheater. "Today you are a man," Tim says.

Cara pinches Karl's cheek, and then they all go their separate ways, for secrecy's sake, leaving Karl with the smell of perfume in his nostrils, intoxicated and alone.

One of his weekly chores is dumping all the little wastepaper baskets in his house into a big trash bag. While he's shaking the bathroom basket and watching the tissues and Q-tips tumble out, he hears his mother venting to his father in the bedroom. "They're like piranhas, they taste a drop of blood and they're all over us."

"What did you tell them?" his father asks. "You can't exactly deny what's standing there in broad daylight."

Karl can't figure out what they're talking about, only that his mother seems to have had another bad day at work. The door opens. They emerge in their evening sweatshirts and freeze at the sight of him.

"What happened?" he asks. "Are you okay?"

She explains on the way to the kitchen. "Paul left me to handle the reporters by myself all day, which is the part of the job I hate the most."

"Why were reporters bothering you?"

"Well. He did something that was a bit . . ."

"Illegal?" Karl's dad suggests.

"Audacious."

"What did he do?"

In the kitchen, his mother pours pistachio nuts into a plastic bag and pounds them on the cutting board with a wooden mallet. They're having Pistachio Pasta for dinner tonight: tortellini with tomatoes, scallions, and nuts, and Parmesan on top. It's Karl's favorite dinner, but other concerns have him too distracted to notice.

"Mom? What did your boss do?"

His father snickers.

"Stop that," Mom grumbles. She keeps hammering as she explains. "He decided to build a few more floors than originally planned."

"Three, to be exact," Dad contributes.

"And the city government is upset because he didn't get approval for the change."

"Also, the lot isn't zoned for a building that tall," Dad adds.

"Meanwhile, it was a slow news day, and the press is all over us."

"But why would he suddenly add three extra floors?" Karl asks.

While his father snickers some more, his mother blushes. "You have to understand, Karl, commercial real estate in New York is worth a lot. Every square foot of it."

"So he broke the law to make extra money?"

"He disagreed with the Planning Commission's decision. He felt the site could easily accommodate thirty-four floors."

Karl has been setting the dinner table; his parents are working in the kitchen. He assumes they won't notice his silence from this distance, but he's wrong.

"Listen," his mother pleads, "I wish he'd just done what he was supposed to do. My life would be much simpler, and my head wouldn't be pounding. But it's his decision, and I can't get on my high horse and condemn him, and I really wish you wouldn't either, because half of everything we own comes from his success at cutting through bureaucracy."

Karl stands mutely with his hand on the fork he has just set down. *She's not sleazy,* he tells himself. *It's her boss, not her.*

"As crimes go, it's really fairly harmless," she says. "He'll pay a big fine and that'll be that."

"He'll probably pay his lawyers more than the fine," Karl's father says.

"And he'll *still* come out ahead. That's the magic of Manhattan real estate."

"Yes, there's a lot of money in dirt."

His father gives Karl a sly grin—and his mother slams a cabinet door shut. "As if *your* clients were model citizens."

"Careful," his father says, grinning nervously. "There are minors present."

"What does she mean?" Karl asks.

"Nothing."

"They just hide all their assets in offshore corporations, that's all. Which Dad sets up for them."

"All according to law."

"But you do have to go to court sometimes, to explain why Bob the Billionaire only paid two hundred dollars in taxes."

"The only time I have to go to court is when the I.R.S. decides to throw a scare into the public. Now could we please change the subject?"

During dinner, Karl's parents misunderstand his unhappiness. They think it's all about *them*, and they go to great lengths to convince him that there's nothing wrong with the work they do. He'd like them to just stop talking, but he can't explain that what's really bothering him is his own dishonesty, not theirs.

He's reading *Die Ilse ist weg* for school and listening to Good Vibes on WUHU (the mellow sound of the vibraphone usually smoothes away his rough edges, but not tonight) when someone or something raps on his bedroom window.

"Nevermore," squawks Matt.

"Come on, Hermit Crab," Lizette calls to him, "we're going to Friendly's."

"I don't think so," Karl mumbles.

"It's okay, we all took showers," Jonah says.

"Sorry, I'm"—umm, not *busy*, but what?—"not feeling that great."

Matt pretends to tear his hair out. "He doesn't like us anymore!"

"What's wrong, Herm?" Lizette asks. "That time of the month?"

"I'm just not in the mood. I'll see you guys tomorrow."

He shuts the window and draws the shade.

They tap on the glass, all three of them in unison, rapidly, persistently, comically. He has to lift the shade and wave them away.

The doorbell rings, of course. Karl's dad lets Lizette in and chats with her briefly before sending her to Karl's room.

"What's up, Carlo?"

"Nothing's up."

She returns to the swamps of Florida, for comedy's sake. "Hold on there, son. The boys and me invite y'all to Friendly's and you turn us down flatter than flounders, and then you say ain't nothin' wrong? Sounds mighty *un-*Friendly to me."

"It's personal, all right? I don't want to talk about it."

Lizette has very little of the therapist in her. Uncomfortable, she jokes, "So, do you want to talk about it?"

He gives her a scowl.

"This wouldn't have anything to do with a certain armrubbing, homework-copying person, would it?"

"No."

She nods, a silent *whew.* "Well—if you decide you want to talk, let me know."

He locks the door after she goes, and wishes there were some small part of what's going on that he could tell her. But there really isn't.

Most of the gloom wears off by morning. Karl eats lunch with the Slightly Irregular Three, and enjoys the story of

the surly waitress at Friendly's that ends with Jonah saying, "Which part of fleppin-slabob-n'gosh didn't you understand?" Life seems generally good again, and after school
the four of them go to the soggy football field at Van Dinky
Park and play Footnis, in which you have to serve the tennis
ball in an arc from behind your team's twenty-yard line—a
game Karl himself invented, and there's much laughter and
diving and panting, that is until Blaine calls Karl over to his
convertible to discuss the next mission.

Mr. Watney, with his reddish goatee, is widely considered
the best teacher in the school. He has a trick of recounting
historical events in the present and even the future tense—
"Over six days, the stock market loses almost a third of its
value. For millions, life savings simply vanish. Comedian
Groucho Marx will lose over two hundred thousand dollars.
He comments later, 'I would have lost more, but that was all
the money I had.'" The Watney style seemed a little weird at
first, but now his students get goose bumps as the stories of
Pearl Harbor and the Scopes Monkey Trial unfold.

Mr. Watney has intellect and charisma, but he also has
one blatant character flaw: vanity. *He primps.* Not only
does he comb his hair during class, he even installed three
mirrors on the back wall of his room, and you can see him
checking himself out from this angle or that during his
roaming lectures. If he could cure this one fault, he would
be magnificent.

But at least he's fair. He tells his students four possible
essay questions in advance of each test, so they can prepare

answers. And he lets them type their tests on their laptops, if they prefer, which is a major kindness to both the nimble typists and the handwriting-challenged.

He also likes to puncture the tension on test days with silliness. He covers the blackboard with a red velvet curtain his mother sewed, and as he pulls the cord, he hums the Olympic fanfare through a blue kazoo. The curtain rises, and there, in pale green chalk, stands today's test question:

WHO WAS MOST RESPONSIBLE FOR THE CUBAN MISSILE CRISIS, THE U.S., THE U.S.S.R., OR CUBA?

Karl outlined answers for all four questions, so now he only needs to turn his sketchy outline into coherent paragraphs. He begins: *If you work backward in time, you'll see that the Cuban Missile Crisis stemmed directly from the many U.S. attempts to assassinate Fidel Castro, or at least overthrow him.*

And so on, through the end of paragraph one, at which point he activates The Plan. Copying the paragraph, he pastes it into an email that he sends to RebGroup, for them to paraphrase.

Who can comprehend the mysteries of the human mind? Why would a person as smart as Karl forget to turn down the volume on his laptop, when the worst thing that could possibly happen would be the loud *blibadip* that alerts Mr. Watney to the fact that someone has just sent an email? Or, to put the question bluntly: does Karl *want* to get caught?

Personally, I don't think so. You're free to think otherwise, though.

Instantly, Mr. Watney raises his eyes to the mirrors in the back of the room. In the center mirror, he sees (partially eclipsed by Karl's shoulder) the email window on Karl's screen.

Mr. Watney twitches—an alarming sight, for this is a supremely confident, unflappable teacher—and says, "Karl, come up here."

Our hero walks the narrow aisle to the front of the room and follows Mr. Watney to the recessed doorway. A desperate glance at Vijay—*What do I do now?!*—goes unreturned.

"Did you just send the question to someone in the next period?" Mr. Watney whispers.

"No, I didn't," Karl replies, pale as a vampire's victim.

"That's good, because I change the questions from class to class. But what *did* you send? Before you say a word, let me warn you—I'm going to ask to see your computer."

Karl can neither speak nor raise his chin from his chest.

"I don't understand. You have absolutely no reason to cheat. I'm hoping there's an innocent explanation."

"There is," says Phillip Upchurch.

P.U., as most students at Lincoln High call him, has come to the doorway to confer with Karl and Mr. Watney as if he had every right to do so. His white shirt collar rises up out of the blazer's darker collar a perfect half-inch all around.

Baffled, slack-jawed, Karl waits to hear what he will say.

"Phillip, this doesn't concern you," Mr. Watney says.

Upchurch keeps his voice down. "Actually, the note he sent was to me." (Here Karl goes into the Lifeboat State: no longer strong enough to lift a pinky to save himself, he floats passively whichever way the tide carries him.) "I wasn't sure if you said to double-space or single-space the essay, and I didn't want to raise my hand and ask such a stupid question out loud. So I emailed Karl. He was just answering my question. That's why he didn't bother to turn his volume down, I'm guessing—he didn't think he had anything to hide."

Mr. Watney frowns. It's a far-fetched tale, but how can he doubt the word of Phillip Upchurch, whom he privately refers to as Pious the Twelfth?

"I see now that it was an error in judgment, and I take full responsibility for my mistake—but I didn't think anyone would ever know. You just need to understand that it would be a gross injustice to accuse Karl of cheating, when he was only trying to answer an innocent question."

A curl of distaste is visible on Mr. Watney's lips, even with the goatee. In Karl's terror, he can't tell what the distaste refers to, and he's afraid it's him. Why P.U. would lie for him he can't begin to guess; but right now the more urgent question is whether or not the keen-minded Mr. Watney will buy Upchurch's load of crap.

"Phillip," he begins, "you have a distinguished career in the law ahead of you. If you can show me the email you sent to Karl, we'll all forget this ever happened. Can you do that?"

Karl's head is feeling lighter and lighter: the brains must be evaporating inside. A minute from now, he'll be on his way to Klimchock's office. He's not sure how much longer he can stay vertical.

"No problem," Phillip says. "Come look."

Magically, Phillip brings up the lifesaving email on his

laptop screen and shows Mr. Watney. *How is he doing this?* Karl wonders. The only possible answer is that Phillip sent the email right after Karl's laptop sounded its near-fatal *blibadip.*

Mr. Watney waves Karl over.

"I owe you an apology," he says, resting his hand on Karl's shoulder. "Now go ahead and finish the test. Let me know if you need extra time."

Karl writes the rest of his essay without passing it along to the Confederacy. Deeply shaken, he keeps his eyes on the screen and ignores the pellets of crumpled paper that bounce off his head.

He ducks away from Vijay and Ian after class, and catches up with Phillip Upchurch on the stairs.

"Why did you do that?" he asks.

Upchurch rolls his eyes. "You're welcome."

Karl says, "Sorry—I meant to thank you. I just don't get it."

"Consider it charity."

Karl still doesn't understand. Why would P.U. want to save him from disaster?

"All right, if you really have to know, I'll tell you—but this is just between you and me. Everyone around here expects you to be the valedictorian, but I'm planning to beat you. What happens if you get expelled? Every moron in the school is going to say, *Phillip wouldn't be the valedictorian if Karl were still here.* So, whatever you were up to in there, I had to save your behind, unpleasant as that was. Now do you understand?"

Bizarre as it sounds, there's no other plausible explanation. "I don't know what to say," Karl murmurs.

"That's because, deep down, you're really dumb. And untalented, too."

Phillip accelerates, leaving Karl behind—stung and confused.

Sometimes it happens this way: you find yourself owing a large debt of gratitude to a nasty jerk. There isn't much you can do about it, except wait for a chance to save his life and erase the debt.

In his garage, installing gear wheels with a screwdriver bit attached to the electric drill, Karl doesn't hear the VW Beetle pull up to the curb. A scent of musk enters his nostrils; he assumes it's a trick of the brain, a memory masquerading as a real fragrance. *If Cara comes to see me, I'll just tell her I'm through with the whole thing.*

"Wow. What's the invention, Mr. Edison?"

He covers the stainless steel dome quick as a flinch (well, not really, because sheets tend to float slowly downward, darn them) and stands before Cara, tongue-tied.

"It looks like a metal turtle with little pipes coming out of its back," she says. "Let's see . . . is it a remote-controlled spy submarine? That shoots poison darts at enemy scuba divers?"

He shakes his head.

"Am I close?"

Another head shake, since he can't speak.

She pats the outer shell through the sheet.

"Goofy and Pluto. Hm. Which is which, anyway? I can never keep them straight."

It occurs to him that she may be a foreign-born secret agent. That would explain the missing vowel in her last name, *Nzada*. Maybe they sent her here to corrupt America's youth.

"So, I assume you're thumbs-down on the cheating thing."

"That's right."

"Understandable, after a near-death experience. A lesser man would've fainted on the spot."

"It's not just about almost getting caught."

"Oh?"

She says this with a sparkle, as if anticipating an extremely creative lie.

He watches his sneaker rub the garage floor. "The dishonesty is bothering me."

"Really?"

She comes closer. He steps backward and bumps against the rim of Project X's shell.

"Tell me more about this—what do you call it? A conscience?"

Annoyed and hyperstressed, he lets loose a flood of misery over his parents' sleazy work, and how he doesn't want to be like that. "I just don't like what I'm doing."

"I have a question," she says. "You're seventeen, right?"

"I will be in a few weeks."

"Close enough. Aren't you a little old to believe in the tooth fairy?"

He sees where she's going, and it disappoints him. Every-thing he said came from the heart. If all she can say in reply is that honesty is a fairy tale, intended only for small children, then she's not as captivating as he thought, because she's trying to sell him a lie—and it's not even an original lie.

Cara responds to his sour face by turning in a new direc-tion. "The whole world is unfair, Karl. It's just a fact of life. Your parents aren't bad people—they're normal. Cheating is just a quick, efficient way to reach your goals. There's no room for purity and virtue once you get a job. Name any career and there are compromises that go with it."

"Doctor."

"I didn't mean *name a job*, Karl, I meant it's a universal thing. But okay, since you don't believe me—let's say you're Dr. Petrofsky, and you know that your sick patient, Mrs. Bobo, needs to stay in the hospital two days, but the HMO says, *Sorry, outpatient surgery. Next!* You argue, you protest, but in the end you do what you're told, because otherwise you're out of business."

He doesn't know if she's right or wrong. How could he know? The only job he's ever held was scooping ice cream last summer at Baskin-Robbins, and the only compromise he had to make was when an entire soccer team came in: a couple times, he didn't dunk the scooper between flavors.

"I don't understand why you should be lecturing me about how the world works. It's not like you're five years older than me."

"Probably it's because you spend your life in a garage. This is all common knowledge, Karl. My dad used to say how funny it is, the way people talk so nobly and meanwhile there's all this thievery and backstabbing going on. He said, 'The ones that preach the loudest are the always the biggest crooks.'"

He wishes he could disprove everything she's saying, but he can't.

"Personally," she adds, "I think it's cool that your mom's boss built those extra floors. That's nerve."

Grimly studying the garage floor, Karl notices the silvery flecks left over from painting his first thermosensitive shingle. Those were the good old days.

"Hey, Edison—don't pout, it makes your mouth look weird."

She prods his skinny midsection (you can't really call it a belly) with her index finger. He fears the long, sharp nail will pierce the skin and draw blood.

"Question," she says. "Did school suddenly get less cruel and unfair than it was yesterday?"

He shakes his head gloomily.

"So let's be honest, since you like honesty. You got scared because you almost got caught. Really, if you peel away all the talk, this is about fear, not lofty principles. It's about nerve—so get some! Like your mom's boss."

A long shelf covered with dusty tools and doodads travels the length of the garage, shoulder high. Karl stares at the jug of blue windshield washer fluid—clinging to it like a shipwrecked sailor bobbing on the waves, just trying to hang on and survive.

She plucks a chocolate crumb from his collar. (Must have been there the whole time, a souvenir of his after-school Mallomars.) "Changing the subject slightly, do you agree that it would be a good thing to act on your desires once in a while, instead of giving up in advance because it's scary and you might get in trouble?"

"I guess I can agree with that."

"Good!"

She leans back against the top tube of his bike, smiling mischievously. Her silver satin shirt shimmers.

She's waiting for something.

"What's going on?" Karl asks nervously.

"I'm giving you a chance to practice."

Karl is roughly as scared as he was when Mr. Watney called him to the front of the room. "What do you mean?"

"Uh-uh-uh. That's a delaying tactic. You know what I mean."

Because he lives on a cul-de-sac, there's not much chance that a car, bike, skateboarder, or knife-wielding psycho will pass by. He has no excuse whatsoever to look anywhere but into Cara's eyes.

She shifts her weight, crosses her ankles the other way. She seems willing to wait indefinitely.

"I don't understand all this," Karl says.

"Yes you do."

"No, I don't. I mean, why are you doing this?"

"Ohhhhh. You think I'm . . . *using* you."

Karl turns his back to her and visits with Goofy. The situation is unbearably humiliating. He can't face her.

"Karl—I'm not using you. Really."

Her hands appear down below, on his waist. Is he still breathing?

"The truth is, I don't care that much if you help us cheat

or not," she says. "There are other reasons why I'm interested in you. Should I name them? Okay. First, you're the only person at school who's as smart as I am—though in a different way. Second, I'm enjoying the whole Shy Guy Comes Out of His Shell thing. There's a definite cuteness about you—the Awkward Genius. It's new for me."

She's still there, behind him, holding his waist, waiting for him to turn and kiss her. Whether or not she really means what she said—honesty means nothing to her, so it's hard to tell—he would be a pathetic coward if he didn't accept the challenge.

Having never kissed a girl before, he goes instinctively for the cheek.

"I'm not your aunt," she says. "Try over this way," and she points to her smile, which seems more amused than adoring.

He finds, when his lips arrive at hers, that he can't believe this is happening. Literally: *it's not real,* a voice in his head keeps saying. She can't like him this way. And what about Blaine, are they together or aren't they?

He pulls away a bit, figuring it's best to end the kiss before she gets bored. Once disconnected, he's at a loss for words.

"Isn't it better to grab what you want?" she asks.

"Yes."

"And are you going to do more of it in the future?"

"Yes."

"That's good. Because shy is only cute up to a point."

There are flecks of gold in her green irises. Those eyes are so beautiful, they inspire him to hope. He wants to become a person she respects, not an entertaining project. He agrees with her: he *has* been cowardly, he *should* be braver. It's time to crack the shell.

He puts both hands in her hair. It's so soft, so fine, he feels he's touching a goddess. Nonetheless—*Courage!*—he kisses her again.

She smiles. "Well done."

Chapter 5

In a survey of high-achieving teenagers a few years back, more than three-quarters admitted that they had cheated in school. Of these cheaters, nine out of ten said they'd *never gotten caught*."

With eighteen teachers jammed into Mr. Klimchock's small office, there's no room for him to pace the floor dramatically. He can't even throw his arms out to the sides, or he'll knock over Mr. Grantley's Diet Pepsi and Ms. Singh's Snapple, perched on opposite edges of his desk. The smell of Mrs. Kazanjian's tuna salad dominates the room; posters for *Man of La Mancha*, *Cats*, *Pippin*, and *Fiddler on the Roof* surround the teachers, making them feel as if they've wandered into the lair of a mad theater fan, for whom time stopped in the 1970s.

"You can't *persuade* students to behave ethically. You

can't tell them that cheating doesn't pay when they see dishonesty rampant in politics and business. In the 1940s, only twenty percent of college students interviewed admitted to cheating in high school. But the world has changed since then."

Mr. Watney gulps down a bite of turkey on rye so he can retort, "The change in numbers may just mean that students answer surveys more honestly now."

The widespread chuckling shows that most of these teachers oppose Mr. Klimchock and his campaign to wipe out cheating—but the assistant principal doesn't need their love or their approval. He lives by the famous words of President Lyndon Johnson, "If you've got 'em by the balls, their hearts and minds will follow."

"As I was saying, schools are the last best hope for restoring honesty to our society. We can't do it with logic or by pleading. But we *can* produce honesty through fear."

The only sound in the room is Mr. Grantley, chomping on his pickle.

From his coat closet, Mr. Klimchock wheels out a mannequin on a rolling desk chair. The mannequin, slumping limply to one side, wears a hooded sweatshirt and sunglasses.

"Know Your Enemy!" Mr. Klimchock blares.

"I have that boy in my algebra class," says Mrs. Kazanjian—an unexpected joke from the famously cranky chess team adviser.

"Did it ever occur to you that he's hiding more than his hair?" Mr. Klimchock asks.

With the flair of a magician yanking a tablecloth out

from under a ten-course banquet, Mr. Klimchock pulls the hood back, revealing headphones on the mannequin's ears. The wires disappear inside the sweatshirt; Mr. Klimchock reaches into the pouch and comes out with a CD player. "What's our little dummy listening to during his biology test?" He pops the player's lid and shows them the CD label: Lethal Doopy, *WA$$UP?* "Let me guess. If you got this far, you would now tell your student, 'I don't know how you can listen to that awful noise,' and that would be that. Am I right?"

"No, I never insult their music. I don't want to sound like my mother."

"Come here and listen, please."

Mrs. Kazanjian threads her way among the knees and feet and chair legs. Mr. Klimchock hands her the head-phones, and she puts them on. When he plays the CD, her jaw drops. "Diploid cell—chromosomes in homologous pairs," she hears. "The diploid number, 2n, equals twice the haploid number."

"This CD was confiscated by a teacher I know in Ho-Ho-Kus. I've been doing my research, you see. They have methods we never heard of ten years ago. You can go back to your seat, Fern."

As Mrs. Kazanjian returns to the back of the room, Mr. Klimchock produces a Thom McAn shoe box from behind his desk. The box is filled with seemingly random objects: a watch, a water bottle, an eyeglass case, a mechanical pencil.

"Now let's see. What's the point of this innocent para-phernalia?"

He dazzles his audience with one amazing revelation after another. Taped to the back of the watch is a teeny-weeny, folded-up cheat sheet. There's a similar index card inside the eyeglass case, hidden behind the lens cloth, and a rolled-up page of physics formulas inside the mechanical pencil, where the extra lead belongs. If you turn the water bottle around, wonder of wonders, you can read a list of Egypt's pharaohs and the monuments each one left behind, with an asterisk for Hatshepsut, the first female pharaoh—all magnified by the liquid inside, all discretely tucked behind the label.

"From now on, the rule prohibiting cell phones will be strictly enforced at Abraham Lincoln High School. Hooded sweatshirts, mechanical pencils, and water bottles with labels are hereby banned. The same goes for mp3 players, graphing calculators, and PDAs."

"Public Displays of Affection?" Ms. Vitello whispers to Herr Franklin.

"Quiet back there," Mr. Klimchock barks. "I expect every one of you to visit these websites tonight, and learn more about how your students have made fools of you."

He hands out a list of sites such as CheatersProsper, CheatStreet, and EZA.com.

Mr. Watney clears his throat.

"All right, let's hear your rebuttal, Timothy."

(Killer instinct: Mr. Klimchock has correctly guessed that Mr. Watney *hates* to be called by his full first name.)

"Some of us have been talking—"

"I see. A mutiny."

"And we agree with you that the cheating has to stop, that it's bad for the school and bad for the students."

"Go on. Plunge your dagger in."

"What we can't agree with is the harshness of the penalty. What you're doing is way out of proportion."

Ms. Singh—a lovely young pistol, full of dazzling white teeth and energetic gestures—dives into the fight head-first. "You have to understand where they're coming from. There's so much pressure on them. If they want to get into a top school, they have to perform at a superhuman level. Not only do they need perfect grades in the hardest subjects, but they also have to excel in an extracurricular activity, and that takes time. The system practically *pushes* them to cheat—it's almost impossible to meet the requirements any other way."

Herr Franklin adds, "Instead of severely punishing them, I think we should have them take a Saturday class in ethics. That way, they might learn something from all this."

"Anyone else?" Mr. Klimchock asks. "Go ahead, this is your big opportunity. Hit me with your best shots. Don't be afraid—what can I do? Fire you?"

The room goes quiet again. No one dares to speak—except frail, white-haired Mrs. Rose, who comments tremulously, "It's just a shame the way everything has gone downhill. Just a shame."

"I agree, Amelia. Things *have* gone downhill—including teachers' understanding of right and wrong. Isn't there anyone else in this room who sees that we have to crush dishonesty?"

Miss Verp, built like a football player but with a pixie haircut and an itty-bitty voice, raises her hand.

"Ah. An ally."

"I've never met a student with a conscience," she pipes sweetly. "Nothing makes an impression on them except severe punishment."

Mr. Klimchock rewards her loyalty with praise—though he despises her for currying favor. "That's the first sensible comment I've heard so far. As for the rest of you, your 'sympathy' and 'understanding' are misplaced. By coddling wrongdoers, you let them thrive and multiply. You might as well fight bacteria by putting them in a damp, warm intestine."

"But you're—"

"When you run this school, Timothy, you can run it your way. Until then, disagree in silence."

"Speaking of running the school," says Ms. Vitello, "where's Mr. Hightower? Why isn't he leading this meeting? Does he know what you're doing?"

These are excellent questions. No one has seen the principal in months. Mr. Fernandez, who joined the staff midyear, right out of college, after Mrs. Langerhans collapsed in the bio lab, has never met Mr. Hightower and isn't convinced that he really exists. (Mrs. Langerhans is doing better now, thanks for asking, and sends greetings to friends and colleagues from her retirement condo in Pompano Beach, Florida.)

"Mr. Hightower has a lunch meeting with the superintendent today," Mr. Klimchock explains. "There are certain staffing issues they need to work out. I wouldn't worry for now—not till we hear something definite. As for your other question, yes, I met with him this week and explained my plans, and he gave me his blessing. I couldn't do this without his support, could I?"

His forced smile leads Mr. Watney to suspect that Mr. Klimchock may be doing the exact thing he's denying, i.e., running this whole reign of terror behind the principal's back. If he could just get the principal alone and ask some questions—

A firm *knock knock knock* on the door derails Mr. Watney's train of thought.

"Open that, please, Charlene," Mr. Klimchock says, frowning at the interruption. Miss Verp obeys.

Standing at the door is a student, someone we haven't met before. Her hair frames her face in a neat, spray-hardened oval. Her gray slacks, with a straight crease down the front of each leg, seem to have been delivered by time machine from a more conservative decade. She wears too much makeup, more than a girl her age needs, including a thick coat of foundation. This leads the women in the room to assume she's covering up acne scars, but in fact, there's nothing underneath the makeup but fierce ambition and a peculiar directness.

"Mr. Klimchock, I'm Samantha Abrabarba," she announces. (Her voice, loud and grating, reminds Mr. Watney of a car engine, backing up fast.) "I'm writing a story for *The Emancipator.* Could I speak to you in private?"

He's about to ask, Can you see that we're in the middle of a meeting?, but she adds, "I'm investigating cheating at school."

Never too busy to hunt his quarry, Mr. K. excuses himself and joins Samantha in the hall.

As soon as the door closes, the murmuring begins.

"He's demented!"

"He's psychotic!"

"How does a person get like that?"

"Obviously he was abused as a child."

"Can't we go to Mr. Hightower and say this has to be stopped?"

"Good luck finding him."

"Then we should go to the superintendent. If the whole teaching staff goes downtown and protests—"

"Whoa, Nelly. I don't know about the rest of you, but there's no way I'm going to complain to the superintendent. I'm too old to start job hunting."

"It doesn't have to be unanimous. Who's willing to go with me to the superintendent's office?"

Four hands go up.

"I can't believe this! You're cowards!"

"What about you, Mr. Grantley? You haven't said a word."

"I'm staying out of it. That's how I've survived here for twenty years. Let the storms rage on the surface; down here the seas are always calm."

"Great. You're an inspiration to us all."

Miss Verp chirps her dissent. "Looks to me like some of you are on the cheaters' side."

"You—you just want Attila the Hun to ask you out."

"It's such a shame, such a shame."

"If we could just—"

And so on. Now you can see why evil madmen and nasty politicians win as often as they do: because everyone else wastes time squabbling instead of uniting to oppose them.

While the teachers bicker among themselves, let's see what's up in the hallway.

"Yes, Miss . . . Abracadabra, was it?"

"Abrabarba. Thank you for taking the time to talk to me."

She whips out a memo pad, bound in black leather, with her initials on the front in gold script, *S.A.*

"Yes, I'm quite interested in this subject, as you know. And I appreciate your coming to see me. Now what information do you have for me in that little black book?"

She opens the pad to a blank page. "I don't have any information yet. I wanted to ask if you've caught anyone since Ivan Fretz, and what you're planning to do next. This is a really important story. If I do a good job, I might be able to sell it to the *New York Times,* as a stringer."

Mr. Klimchock exhales slowly through his nostrils, venting his disappointment. "In other words, you'd like to publish my plans and alert the student body so they can take the necessary precautions."

"I—*what*?! Are you kidding? I *hate* cheaters. I'd like to see them all expelled. That's why I'm doing this story—to expose them."

"I see. Well, then, maybe we can help each other. Keep your eyes and ears open. Be cagey—don't go around announcing what you're up to. If you hear anything that could be useful, share it with me. And I promise, in return, if I have any news to report, I'll give you the scoop. How's that for a deal?"

"Okay, but are you sure you can't tell me anything right now?"

He considers giving her a dramatic quote, something along the lines of "Let the cheaters be warned, the day of reckoning is near." In the end, though, he sticks with his No

Comment strategy. The goal, after all, is to catch them, not to scare them straight.

"I'm sorry, but secrecy is essential."

She jots those words on her pad.

"But you *do* have a plan, right? Is that what you're meeting about in there?"

It's not hard to imagine Samantha, a few years down the road, thrusting a microphone in a disgraced senator's face and asking, When did you first start taking bribes to support your drug habit?

"I have to ask you," Mr. Klimchock says, with as much paternal benevolence as he can simulate, "not to even mention my plans. If you do, you'll compromise the entire effort."

"But that's a violation of freedom of the press. You can't ask me not to do the story."

"I'm not *ordering* you to be silent. I'm *asking* you, as a citizen of this school, not to tip off the bad guys. Talk it over with Mr. McPune, he's your faculty adviser."

Note to self, Mr. Klimchock thinks. *Threaten McPune later. The paper can't print one word about this.*

Back in his office, with only a few minutes left in the period, Mr. Klimchock booms, "Finishing up. Our goal right now is to capture as many of the enemy as possible, and make examples of them. To do that, we're going to set a trap. This weekend, when the building is empty, technicians will install hidden video cameras in each of your classrooms. No matter what personal opinions you may hold"—he sears Mr. Watney and Ms. Singh with two consecutive glares— "you will keep this plan secret. You WILL NOT warn the students about the cameras, because you will remember which side you're on. If that's not enough, I'll add one more encouragement: if any of you tell your students in spite of my warnings, I'll find out, and you'll find yourselves not only unemployed, but unemployable. Even the all-powerful teachers' union can't protect people who aid and abet cheaters."

Sensing that the others aren't quite as exhilarated as he is—Ms. Singh has her head in her hands and she's shaking it from side to side—he shifts gears and tacks on an inspiring conclusion. "This isn't forever, my good instructors. It's just a surgical strike. We'll rid ourselves of the creeping menace and terrify the others so thoroughly that they'll walk the line for the rest of their lives. Just as Herr Franklin hoped, this will be a valuable educational experience. The floor is about to drop from beneath the feet of some very deserving students—and I wouldn't be surprised if we find some unexpected faces caught in our net. Honesty *will* prevail at Lincoln High. Thanks for coming, everybody."

As the teachers file out—their opposition expressed only in the noisy clenching of paper bags—Mr. Klimchock pops the CD of *Guys and Dolls* into his boom box. They're out in the hall by the time he starts singing along, but they can hear his vigorous, piercing tenor, "When you see a guy reach for stars in the sky . . ."

Chapter 6

Just another ordinary AP calculus test, $\int(2\sec^2 x - 5\csc^2 x)dx$. A bit hard to make it out, though, because of the weird angle. Next time they definitely have to find a better place for the camera than Karl's wrist.

"What's that?" Vijay asks, pointing to a tiny squiggle on his laptop screen. "Does it say 'squared' or 'cubed'?"

"Can't tell," Noah replies—but Karl, sixty yards away in Mr. Imperiale's classroom, obligingly shifts his hand, and the itty-bitty exponent is revealed to be a 2.

Blaine's parked car sways. It's Cara, leaning against the door. "Is this study hall?" she asks through the window.

"Ssh! The test is next period," Blaine says as the three scholars industriously copy Karl's solution onto their tiny cheat sheets.

Upstairs, meanwhile, Karl performs his role so smoothly

that Mr. Klimchock, studying the monitor in his office, detects nothing.

There's one hairy moment, though, when Mr. Imperiale hovers over Karl as he works. The hairiness is due to the fact that Karl's shirt cuff has slipped back a centimeter, revealing the front end of the small black camera.

As soon as he notices, Karl starts to sweat. He must hide the camera without calling attention to it, immediately.

Inspired, he yawns and stretches—not with his arms up in a Y, but down at his sides. Shaking his wrists a bit, a plausible finale to the yawn, he gets the cuff to slide back down over the camera.

"Uh-oh," Mr. Imperiale says, freezing the blood in Karl's veins. "If you're yawning, I guess I'd better come up with some tougher questions next time."

Karl leaves his left arm dangling over the edge of his desk, hiding the bulge in his cuff. "No, I was just up late last night."

"Good for you! Human computer AND party animal. Breaking the stereotype, twenty-four seven. You wild and crazy guy."

The teacher moves on, murmuring to Conor Connolly, "Remember the Power Rule"—leaving Karl to finish the test and the transmission in peace.

Climbing the hill toward Sunrise Place that afternoon, past the diamond in Blortsmek Park where a girls' softball game is in progress, Karl worries that he should have worn different clothes. Cara will be there: what will she think of his dull box-check shirt and his ill-fitting jeans?

Once he sees which house is Blaine's, other worries take over. It's the really big one, made of gray stone, with the giant sloping lawn and the brick driveway that swoops up the hill and around behind. His whole life, Karl has wondered who lived here, and what did they do with all those rooms. (Dive into mounds of gold coins?) But now he's going to a party here, and his sneakers suddenly look unacceptably soiled, the once-white rubber pathetically worn in front and coming off a bit, and there are frayed threads at the bottoms of his jeans.

The only path from the driveway to the front door consists of a few small squares of slate set in the grass. It rained this morning, and the lawn is still wet, and now so are his sneakers, from scuffing over the grass.

Blaine opens the door, chuckling, and explains that no one actually uses this entrance. If Karl feels a bit foolish, the foolish feeling fades fast in the face of the furnishings within. The marble floor gleams, the staircase is a spiral; the life-size photorealist paintings show men in suits doing ordinary things like sneezing and blowing a bubble-gum bubble. Everything here reflects light, dustlessly. When Blaine asks him to take off his wet sneakers, Karl obeys instantly.

Familiar but incongruous noises from the basement prepare Karl for the sight of Blaine's amazing antique Fun Land, featuring Skee-Ball, arcade bowling (you know, the kind where you slide the steel puck and the pins fall up instead of down), Ping-Pong, foosball, a pool table, darts, and six friends enjoying themselves.

Inserting a dime in the old Coke machine, Blaine takes

the glass bottle from behind the little window and hands it to Karl. "All hail our honored comrade," he announces, putting his hand on Karl's shoulder. Tim tootles a trumpet fanfare on his fist, and the Confederates interrupt their play to hoist their beverages.

"We thank you, Karl," Blaine says, "for all you've done, and more importantly, for all you're going to do. Your smartness is matched only by your generosity."

"For he's a jolly good cheater," they sing, which inspires Karl to inspect his sock toes.

That's about it for hoopla. The gathering is low-key, and more comfortable than Karl expected. Alcohol, drugs, cigarettes—there are none to be found here. The party actually seems wholesome. Tim and Ian are smashing the Ping-Pong ball as hard as they can, a comic sight until Ian's paddle whams the table and breaks. ("Oops—sorry, old chap," he tells Blaine.) SCHOOL IS PUNISHMENT FOR THE CRIME OF BEING YOUNG, says Noah's T-shirt; he banks Skee-Balls off the left wall of the ramp as he describes his career plans (study Chinese, get recruited by the CIA, destroy the agency from the inside), while Vijay, his audience, chuckles and slides the steel puck. Cara dances sinuously as she aims her darts, like a soft reed in slow-moving water.

Ever since that afternoon in his garage, Karl has obsessed over the question, What to do about Cara? Obvious Answer Number One: call her and invite her to go someplace with him. But wouldn't she disdain any destination he could think of? Finally, he called his cousin Michelle at NYU for advice, and she, who lived in town for most of her life, suggested Café EnJay, which has live music and Italian desserts—but when he got up the nerve to call Cara, he couldn't find her last name in the phone book. He could have asked Blaine for her number, but there was that lingering confusion about whether they used to be a couple and maybe still were, sort of. He could have talked to Cara in school, but somehow that seemed like a step in the wrong direction—after those kisses, to stand by the lockers and fumblingly ask her for a date. It just felt backward.

Having exhausted every excuse known to man, in other words, he finds himself a mere six feet away from her, watching her sway slinkily and throw darts. He knew this moment would come when Blaine invited him, and he welcomed the opportunity—in the abstract. In the flesh, things are trickier.

"Hey, stranger. How's your dart game?"

"Don't know. I never tried."

"Then you might turn out to be the best player in the world. Let's find out."

His first dart hits the outermost wire and falls off the board.

"The secret," she says, "is to throw it with the pointy end in front."

All of Cara's darts stick in the board, which is more than Karl can say about his. What was that she said in his garage? *Act on your true desires.* It's hard to know exactly what his true desires are, under this pressure. Maybe he should put his arm around her. No, he can't, not in front of everyone. He may lose his chance by doing nothing, though. The window of opportunity is coming down fast, and he's got his fingers on the sill.

The Confederacy rescues him from his worries with much-needed distraction. Blaine brings around a wicker tray full of goodies, including potato chips that break oh-so-delicately between Karl's teeth, cookies still warm from the microwave, and chocolate mint squares with the manufacturer's logo engraved on the top of each individually wrapped brick. "Someday," says Vijay, chewing, "students will cheat with bionic chips implanted in their eyes."

"I predict it'll happen by 2020," Tim says. "Get it? 2020?"

Vijay and Noah give him the look that groans, *Laaaa-aaaame.*

"Anyone see Mark Madson's tattoo?" Ian asks.

No one has.

"It's so idiotic: a little dragon on his shoulder. I can't believe my former best friend thinks a dragon tattoo is cool."

"Zack Barone used to be my best friend," Blaine says, "and now he has so many piercings, he looks like an acupuncture chart."

"Your taste has obviously improved," Vijay comments.

Cara surprises Karl by joining in. "I found out my friend Sheryl, at my old school, was telling my secrets to everyone. Know how I caught her?"

"How?" Karl asks, tossing a dart that sticks in the wall paneling.

"I told her I had a rare medical condition that was making my breasts swell up. The next day, half the school was staring at my chest."

"That proves nothing," Ian says.

"So, I guess she's not your friend anymore," Karl says.

"I don't believe in friends anymore."

There isn't time to question this startling statement, because Tim quickly seconds it: "A best friend is just a disappointment waiting to happen."

In the sudden stillness, Ian flings a potato chip at Tim's face, Frisbee-style, and says, "Bite fast."

Tim does, though not fast enough.

"One thing's guaranteed," Vijay says. "When you think you can count on someone, that's when they let you down."

"Or they just don't *get* it," Noah grumbles.

Karl's head feels like it's under murky water. Here they are, bad-mouthing the whole idea of friends—but aren't *they* all friends?

He ventures a quiet quip. "If you don't have friends, who'll tell you your breath smells like rotten bananas?"

Blaine bursts out laughing. "You never know what this guy'll say next."

It feels good to bask in the warmth of Blaine's appreciation—and even better when he says, "Hey, Karl, come upstairs with me, I want to show you something. Cara— you too."

Leaving their darts on the pool table, Karl and Cara follow their host up the stairs. Karl wonders if the others resent this preferential treatment. (Was each of them the new guy once, the favorite?) He also wonders if Blaine knows about him kissing Cara and will suddenly turn around and punch him in the nose.

They end up behind the house, between the swimming pool and the greenhouse, in the hot tub. Blaine lends Karl a baggy bathing suit, while Cara reclines daringly in her underwear. The air at head level is cold and damp, but from the neck down, Karl floats deliciously in hot, swirling water. *We're chillin' in the hot tub,* he thinks. The funky, Cloroxy smell keeps the experience from being pure heaven—and you can't exactly call it relaxing to see this much of Cara—but then she rests her ankle across his shins, an alcohol-free form of intoxication. She wouldn't do that if she were anything to Blaine, right?

"It really smells today," Blaine says. "My parents are so insane about spa hygiene. I think they intentionally double the disinfectant tablets."

Karl's head is lighter than usual. Between the hot water and the possibly toxic fumes, maybe he ought to be concerned about passing out and sinking below the surface.

"My mom is the opposite," Cara replies. "I don't think she's ever cleaned the bathtub since I was born. I started doing it myself."

"How do they get so strange?" Blaine muses. "It's like amnesia strikes when they hit thirty, and they forget the whole concept of being normal."

Cara's laughing, Blaine's laughing, and Karl notices that he alone hasn't exposed some ridiculous secret of his parents'. Not that it's required, but he's clearly behind. To truly belong to this inner circle, he must reveal something stupid about Mom and/or Dad. Trouble is, he doesn't want to—and besides, nothing comes to mind.

"My dad was talking about the Nobel Prize at supper last night," he finally says. "He handed me a picture of the gold medal. He said I need to get more focused, so he'll still be alive when I win. The scary part is, he meant it seriously."

Blaine snorts. "We would never put that kind of pressure on you, Karl. All we ask is the right answers, from now till June."

"I'll do my best," Karl says.

"We can't ask any more than that."

Cara strokes the bottom of his foot with the end of her big toe. "Bet you didn't expect to be here a month ago," she says.

Good thing Karl's head is attached to his shoulders. Otherwise it would float away.

Down on the diamond in Blortsmek Park, meanwhile, Lizette has just had the roughest day of her softball career. Though ranked by a scout as one of the five best high school windmill pitchers in the state, she just couldn't hit the corners today, and it was all Karl's fault. Early in the game, she saw him heading up the hill; she watched from the mound, between pitches, as Blaine let him in. There just isn't room in one teenage brain for total game focus *and* preoccupation with a close friend's suspicious doings. Alone and distracted inside the chalk circle, she went through her routine before the next pitch—deep breath, nose wiggle, right foot shake—but she put the ball in the dirt, which you really don't want to do with a runner on base, and then (the runner having advanced to second), she couldn't shake it off, she walked the next two batters, even with the team chattering support and the coach calling out, "Get better, Lizette," until finally Mr. Rubinoff came out to see what the heck was going on, and she couldn't say, *I'm worried about my best friend's soul,* so she just shrugged and popped a piece of Orbit gum in her mouth, her preferred tranquilizer. Mr. Rubinoff didn't give her as hard a time as he might have; he said, "Talk to yourself, Lizette. You're our inspiration, you're our engine. You know better than to linger on a bad pitch. Tell yourself: *nothing but strikes*. Get fired up!" And it worked, she put the next ball right over the middle and didn't give up a grand slam the way she feared, just a high pop-up between second and third, and she crossed the grassless dirt infield for it but didn't see Sarah Leone, the shortstop, coming in, too, until Mr. Rubinoff screamed, *"CALL IT,"* in response to which both girls shouted, "I got it!" and then collided, and all of the Lincoln Presidents jumped up and down in their blue and black shirts, a team-wide tizzy, as the fluorescent green ball rolled away and two of the Pumas crossed home plate.

Neither girl got hurt—Lizette helped Sarah up, Sarah apologized, and Lizette said, "No, it was my stupid fault" (*really* annoyed at Karl now, blaming him for this whole slapstick humiliation) and this time Mr. Rubinoff just said tersely, "Get in the game, Lizette"—which stung, because no one on the team was ever half as *in the game* as she was, usually.

She got out of the inning by luck, not skill (the last batter swung at a wild pitch), but managed to drive in three runs with a triple, and her attitude settled down after that.

The game's over now. (The Presidents won, as always.) Lizette loads the bases into the coach's trunk and turns down her usual ride with Natasha Swenson. The convoy of parent vehicles pulls away from the field as Lizette heads up the hill toward Blaine's house, alone.

No signs of life come from the enormous stone mansion—except for a laugh in the backyard.

Heading straight up the driveway, she arrives at the palatial rear end of the house, with its terraced hillside, its Egyptian gods holding up globe lights along the tiled stairs, and its border of tall, regularly spaced, skinny poplars.

She pauses in amazement beside the greenhouse and hears Karl say, "My dad was talking about the Nobel Prize at supper last night."

You'd have to know Lizette even better than her friends know her to understand why Karl's gentle mockery gives her guts a twist. You see, her mother died when she was in third grade, and her father, a college football coach, has raised her and her brothers by himself ever since. In Lizette's world, you don't speak disrespectfully about your father, EVER. And here's Karl, exposing an embarrassing private conversation with his dad, one of the few people she's met since moving here from Florida who made her feel welcome, who seemed *happy* his son was friends with her. Suffice it to say that she's deeply disappointed in Karl.

It gets worse. When she hears Blaine say, *All we ask is the right answers, from now till June,* tears pool in Lizette's eyes. Not tears of grief—we're talking anger here. Okay, with a little grief mixed in.

She can't confront Karl, though. You can't accuse someone if you can't stand to look at his face.

After a quick shower, during which Cara calls in teasingly, "Hey, why'd you lock the door?" Karl heads back home—on foot, since Cara has to pick her mother up from work. It's a mile-and-a-half walk, so he has plenty of time to plan his next move. Tomorrow, at the Lincoln Day Celebration (postponed from Lincoln's birthday because the painters still hadn't finished the auditorium), he'll grab the seat next to Cara's, and during the pageant, he'll hold her hand. (Or would she consider that terminally uncool?) Anyway, as the festivities are reaching a climax, he'll invite her to Café EnJay. That's the plan—final—no backing out.

Lizette is sitting at the top of his front steps when he gets home. She's staring at him with a blank face that's so unlike her, he might not have recognized her without the dirty uniform and the glove.

The cinnamon-colored dirt on her cheek is streaked with drip marks that he hopes are sweat.

"Are you okay?" he asks.

She keeps her voice down. "At first I thought I wouldn't ever talk to you again, because you're nothing but slime. Then I thought, *Let him try to talk his way out of it. I'll listen to his bull, and then I'll know I was right, he's a lying disgrace and I can't be friends with him anymore.* So go ahead—let me hear your excuses. Come on, I'm waiting."

Confused and alarmed, he assumes this must have something to do with Cara—but he can't figure out what, exactly.

"What are you talking about?"

"'All we ask is the right answers, from now till June.'"

Karl has been worrying about this ever since he joined the Confederacy: *what'll I do if someone catches me?* Interestingly, getting found out doesn't feel like the end of the world. He tells himself he always knew it would happen.

Still, he can't look Lizette in the eye.

"How'd you ever get mixed up with them, Karl? I bet they used Cara as bait. *Here, dumb fishy, look at me wiggle.*"

That touches a nerve. Maybe she's right. Is he the world's biggest idiot, to believe a word Cara said?

"I thought you were a good person. How could you let them talk you into this?"

He needs to puff himself up if he's to defend himself. Annoyed—okay, angry—he says, "Do you think I'm doing it to help myself? Don't you remember what Klimchock did to Ivan? School is an unfair place—this is just a way of hitting back. It's like rebelling against a vicious system."

She stares at him as if he'd recited the Gettysburg Address in Portuguese. "What kind of logic is that? Klimchock's a mean old crud-head, so you'll make the world a better place by cheating? That's like protesting a war by pissing in the reservoir—one thing doesn't have anything to do with other."

"You're not listening. The whole system of grades isn't for our benefit—it's to sort people out. Some go to Yale, others get to collect the garbage. Is that fair?"

"I can almost see what you're saying, but—so what? You cheating doesn't help anybody."

She's making him angrier by the second. She doesn't *want* to understand—and now he can't remember the words Noah used, which made perfect sense at the time.

"You don't have to make such a big deal out of it," he says. "Most people at school cheat, one time or another."

"Says who? *I* don't cheat. And till now I didn't know any-one else who did."

"Well, it's going on, whether you know it or not."

Her big dark eyes won't let go of him. This isn't what friends usually do. Usually, friends see things from your point of view and sympathize; they don't blast you out of the water like a shotgunned duck.

He'd like to go inside and not see her again for a long time—but he can't, because she's blocking the way.

"Karl," she says, and even in the shadow of her visor, he can see her eyes soften, "my dad taught me about cheating a long time ago. You know what he said? He said it's a mat-ter of pride. He said, 'I don't care if it's moving the ball one more inch away from the wall in minigolf—you don't cheat. Ever. Because once you open that door, it gets easier and easier to open it again, till you turn into a different person— sneaky and low, never doing the things you're supposed to do.' Maybe you think you can't say no to these people, but you're wrong. You can."

She's watching him like a searchlight. Even though she still hasn't gotten the point—*he's not doing this to get ahead unfairly*—explaining again won't help.

"You gonna say something? Or are you too ashamed to open your mouth?"

Here's where Karl makes a bad mistake. The second the words leave his lips, he recognizes how stupendously dumb they are, but by then it's too late.

"Are you going to report us?"

She throws her mitt at his face. He ducks to the side; it cartwheels along the concrete walk behind him.

"You need to face up to what you're doing, Karl. Look yourself in the eye and be honest about it."

She stands up. Since she's on the second step from the top, she towers over him like Moses on the mountain.

"What do you want me to say? That I promise never to do it again and please forgive me?"

"Yeah, that'd be a good start. Just *stop*, Karl. Don't let her play you like a harmonica. Get a spine!"

He's never seen Lizette this angry before. It's frightening: all that passion aimed straight at him, criticizing him, instead of teasing him playfully.

She pushes past him and gives his shoulder a shove. "Don't talk to me again unless you quit. I'm serious."

Wait, he wants to call out, but he can't say *Wait* unless he also says, *I'll stop*—and, after this afternoon in the hot tub, he's not ready to do that.

But what's this agonized urge to run down the street and physically keep her from leaving? What's *that* all about?

The blue and black uniform gets smaller and smaller, until she turns the corner and disappears behind Mr. Miyasaki's pear tree. There's an odd, acrid scent in his nostrils, which confuses him. Does torment smell?

No, it's just a leftover trace of funky Clorox.

Chapter 7

Below the stage, the orchestra tunes up, melodious as a car alarm. The heavy green curtain ruffles, bumped by unseen bodies. Abraham Lincoln peeks out, stage left, shielding her eyes from the lights. (Is that Juliette Chang behind the beard?) Karl is a couple minutes late—locker jam—and he can't see Cara anywhere. A waving hand from the far right signals him, *Sit here*—it's Jonah, next to Matt— and Lizette, too, glancing, scowling, looking away.

Karl sweeps the auditorium with his gaze, pretending he didn't see.

"Sit down," Miss Verp commands, sweetly smiling. "You're impeding traffic."

Crushed and defeated, he slips into an aisle seat. So much for resolutions.

"Mind if I join you?" Cara asks and slips past him,

into the seat next to his, leaving a perfumed breeze behind.

"I'm glad you made it, I paid a fortune for these seats," he ad-libs, thrilled at his own quick wit.

She rubs her arm against his, saying, "Good work, Petrofsky. Keep it up."

Suddenly, the future is all sunshine.

They murmur discreetly about this and that. Cara comments that Miss Verp has a strange admiration for kings and dictators. Karl says, "I think she wishes the American Revolution turned out the other way."

The lights go down, the orchestra plays "The Battle Hymn of the Republic," and an African-American Abraham Lincoln slips out between the curtains, spotlit. Applause, a few piercing whistles, some jocks chanting, "A-bie! A-bie!"— same as last year, when Jonah commented, "That's as far as they got in the alphabet"—and then the celebration begins, with reenacted scenes from Lincoln's life. The outgrown buckskin breeches look hilarious on Brett Handshoe, the basketball player, but the slave mother crying as her babies are sold makes Karl's heart squeeze, even though the babies are dolls. Cara's fingertips walk discreetly over the armrest to his leg. "Mind if I visit?" "I'm okay with that." Her fingers drum on his leg as if to say, *This is so boooooooring;* the hand vanishes each time Miss Verp cruises by. When Honest Abe walks three miles to pay back the six cents he overcharged a customer, Cara asks, "Would you do that for me, Karl?" and he answers, "I would walk *six* miles to give you *three* cents. And I'd bring you a cookie."

He's quite pleased with himself, and a bit drunk on her perfume—but now comes the hard part, asking her out. There's Lizette across the auditorium, glaring at him and looking away fast, while a new Lincoln proclaims, "Whenever I hear anyone arguing for slavery, I feel a strong impulse to see it tried on him personally," and then comes the Gettysburg Address, and the Emancipation Proclamation, and the Malice Toward None and Charity for All speech, and Karl knows his fear is ridiculous, since she's done everything humanly possible to encourage him, but what if she's just fooling around, flirting for fun, and she doesn't really mean it?

John Wilkes Booth sneaks up behind the president. Karl knows that it's now or never, the whole assembly won't last another five minutes. As the loud shot sounds and Antonio Feferman slumps forward, Karl responds to the cap gun as if it were a starter's pistol. He cuts off Cara's mockery ("Where's the blood, I want to see blood") and asks, "Want to go to Café EnJay with me, Friday night?"

"Oh," she says, "I told Leo DiCaprio I'd go dancing with him," and Karl—assassinated—can't make his vocal apparatus work again until she adds, "You're so gullible. It's cute! What time will you pick me up?"

A chorus line of high-kicking Lincolns in stovepipe hats, tights, and tap shoes crosses the stage, singing. Instead of "One—singular sensation," they sing, "One—undivided nation—and you can forget the war."

The shock of it (a joke! at school! on the stage, on Lincoln Day!) lifts Karl to new heights of joy. He's so happy that,

when Miss Verp grabs his arm and says, "You—no talking—go stand in the back," he doesn't mind. He floats up
the aisle contentedly, on his own private cloud.

Friday night is a different story. Profoundly nervous, he says
not a word at dinner. His mother doesn't notice, she's too
tangled up in cell phone calls from her boss, and his father
is in Houston on business, so Karl has all the mental space
he needs for visions of bliss and catastrophe.

He's taking a practice SAT at his computer—or, he would
be if he weren't staring blankly at the two-inch souvenir
bust of Ben Franklin on the shelf above—when his mother
passes his doorway and notices something amiss. "Are you
feeling all right?"

His failure to respond clinches the diagnosis. "Okay," his
mother says, "who is she?"

That wakes him up.

"Who's who?"

"The girl you're pining over."

He debates internally: to spill, or not to spill? "I have a
date tonight," he says sheepishly. "I'm a little nervous."

His mom's grin shows only a fraction of her pleasure.
"What are you going to wear?"

He hadn't thought about that. He's stumped. Calculus he
can do; fashion is another matter entirely.

"Let's look in your closet together. This is going to be
fun!"

While standing at the open closet door, contemplating,
she asks, "Do you need me to drive you? Or would that
embarrass you?"

"I was planning to walk. We're just going to Café EnJay, downtown."

"Good. Do you have enough cash?"

"I have twenty dollars."

She hands him two more twenties from her pocket and proceeds to think of one useful tip after another. "You want to sit as far from the speakers as possible, so you don't have to shout at each other to hear. By the way, is this anyone I know?"

"No, I just met her recently."

Next she ventures beyond helpful hints, into the realm of insanity. "You should think about conversation topics in advance. Keep the talk flowing, keep it sparkling—but don't be scared of brief silences, don't rush in and fill them with nervous babble."

"Okay, I won't. Can we figure out what I should wear now?"

"One more thing. My mother used to tell me, 'Be a good listener,' so I would just sit there pretending to hang on my date's every word while he blabbed on and on. That's just baloney. *You* be a good listener, too. Go back and forth— you'll both be happier in the long run."

"This is getting a little weird, Mom."

"Should you bring her a little gift? What does she like?"

Even as he pleads with her to stop, he realizes unhappily that he has no idea what Cara likes, other than darts, perfume, and cheating.

"Remember, fifteen percent tip for adequate service, twenty for excellent. It makes a good impression if you seem like you know what you're doing."

By this time, he has a strong urge to lock his mother in the closet and run away. "Could we just pick my clothes? Please?"

The lineup of box-checked and plaid shirts thoroughly depresses him. The shirts practically sing, *You're a nerd, you're a freak, you're a hopeless goofy geek.* But he's not about to put on Dad's Hawaiian shirt, and it's too late to study Blaine's wardrobe. He's stumped, and bereft of hope.

"May I make a suggestion?" his mother asks.

"Mm-hm."

She removes from the closet the blazer he wore last summer at Grandma Irma's and Grandpa Barney's golden anniversary party, and then slips his green box-checked shirt, still on its hanger, inside the blazer.

"What about pants and shoes?" he asks.

"You won't need those."

His blank face elicits clarification: "Don't you have a sense of humor? Just keep your jeans and sneakers on and let's see what we're working with."

The shirt and blazer over the jeans and sneakers look surprisingly good in the hallway mirror—or, possibly he looks stupid. He can't tell for sure.

"*Voilà!* You're hip!" his mother says.

Having paid zero attention to clothing for the past sixteen years, he can't remember seeing anyone dressed like this. Also, he's grown since last summer, and his arms stick out of the blazer's sleeves a bit too far—almost as much as Brett Handshoe's, playing young Abe Lincoln.

Or Frankenstein's.

While dubiously studying his reflection, he feels a tug on his hair. His mother, with scissors, has a brown curl in her fingers. "It was sticking out right there. Don't worry, I fixed it."

Annoyed and grateful at the same time, he asks, "You think I look okay?"

"My honest opinion? You could use a haircut. Other than that, you're Prince Charming."

Her beaming smile tells him that her judgment can't be trusted.

The gods must be on his side: they have provided, for his first official date, the first warm night in April. As he walks along the gravel path through Swivel Brook Park, the prettiest place in town, he watches the ducks paddle serenely on the stream, and listens to the quiet little waterfall—but it's no use, nothing can calm his pounding heart or put the strength back in his rubbery legs.

Still, he tries to appreciate this beautiful night, and the bright sliver of moon. If he can just think positive (instead of worrying endlessly that Cara will change her mind about him due to his nervous uncoolness), this may turn out to be the best night of his life.

It might not be a bad idea to take Mom's advice and think of some conversation topics. He could ask if she has any idea what she wants to do as a career—or what colleges she's thinking about—or if she has any pets, or brothers and sisters. (Starting to panic here.) Did she ever take music lessons? If she were stranded on a desert island, what three coconuts, I mean books, would she want with her?

He's boring her to death already, and he hasn't even said hello yet.

Cara lives at 650 State Street. He knows this because he has the address on a slip of paper, and he's taken it out of his pocket thirteen times since leaving home. To reach number 650, he has to go down the slope, past the railroad tracks and the car wash. The creepiness of this deserted neighborhood harmonizes perfectly with his anxiety.

When he arrives at number 650, it's a dry cleaner. Maybe he has the number wrong? No—a fourteenth glance confirms the address. Did she send him here as a cruel joke?

No, she didn't. Next to the dry cleaner is another door, which also says 650.

Inside, there's nothing but mailboxes, and a flight of steps covered by a worn brown carpet. The one light at the top of the stairs doesn't really do the job. He hopes he won't find a murderer hiding at the top of the stairs.

What did his mother tell him? Listen when she talks. Don't sit near the speakers.

The doorbell may not work—or else they can't hear it inside because of the music, an old song playing extremely loud. *"Do you really want to hurt me? Do you really want to make me cry?"*

His polite knock doesn't stand a chance. Regretfully, he pounds on the door like the FBI.

Smoke hits him in the face when the door opens. Cara's mother, a slender woman in tight white pants and a magenta satin blouse, has a glass of wine in her hand. Behind her, at a folding table with metal legs and a Monopoly game in progress, a heavyset, black-haired guy sits and smokes, red-faced. There are posters of the Matterhorn and the Eiffel Tower on the walls, plus a fuzzy poster of cats fishing.

Cara's mom looks a lot like her except that her mom's hair is short and sandy blond and swoops down over one eye. Indian bangles jangle on both of her wrists. "Yeeeeeees?" she asks, having fun.

"Hi. Is Cara home?"

"No, she went out a while ago."

The English language has several words for Karl's state of mind. Disconcerted. Flustered. Discombobulated. Flummoxed. My personal favorite is *nonplussed*.

"I was supposed to—I told her I'd pick her up at seven-thirty."

"Oh. Hm." She makes a series of quizzical expressions. "That's odd. You're saying you had a date with her?"

Did she just say it was odd that Cara agreed to go out with him?

"Yes."

"Well. Wow."

The guy at the table takes a long drag on his cigarette, holding it between his thumb and index fingertip. He shakes his head at Karl slowly, sympathetically, as if to say, Tough break, kid.

A striped cat leaps up on the table and walks across the Monopoly board without disturbing a single house or hotel.

"Do you think she'll be back in a minute or two?"

"No, I really don't think so. Because—this is awkward,

isn't it?—she left with another young man. How long ago was that, Wendell?"

"Twenty minutes."

Karl gropes for understanding, in vain.

"She must have just forgotten. Sorry—what's your name, so I can yell at her for standing you up?"

"Karl."

As he speaks the syllable, his name sounds fatally lame to him—the kind of name you'd have if you were born to be forgotten, blown off, laughed at.

"Don't let it get you down, Karl. She's a little flaky sometimes. I'll tell her you stopped by, okay?"

Silent and immobile, Karl stands in the carpeted hallway, a statue of himself.

"You have a good night, Karl," the man says from the table as the door closes.

He can't remember descending the stairs. All he knows is, he's wandering up State Street like the ghost of a slain soldier, back the way he came.

When he gets to Swivel Brook Park, instead of turning toward home, he keeps going on State—floating uphill, past the fire station and the Laundromat, too destroyed to think—or no, that's not right, because his brain *is* working, it takes all his mental strength to keep it aimed away from Cara, who didn't care enough about him to remember they had a date. He searches for distraction in the windows of the Chinese and Indian restaurants, and then, farther up the hill, the Thai, Cajun, and French restaurants—and then the antique shops, and the four stone banks at the corner of Park—the same way he would have walked with Cara. Maybe it's his own fault, he delayed too long and someone else sneaked in ahead of him. (Is it someone he knows?)

This might be a good time to consider Lizette's advice. *Get a spine.* It wasn't just Klimchock's tyranny that made him join the Confederacy, was it?

Café EnJay has a painted red coffee cup on its window, from which wavy lines of steam rise. A waitress leads two people to a window table inside; the red cup eclipses their heads, but when they sit, Karl sees that the girl is Cara and the guy is some kind of rock star–looking person in his twenties, wearing a sleeveless black T-shirt to show off his muscles. This guy has short, rumpled, blond hair and a matching mustache. Even from across the street and through glass, Karl can see that his eyes are intensely blue, and that Cara is enjoying their blueness.

She takes a break from drinking in the splendor of her rock star's face, and glances out the window. Karl turns his back so fast that his blazer's tail whips around. He keeps going up State, head turned unnaturally to the right—but peeks back after a few steps, unable to resist. Instead of Cara in the window, he spots Lizette, Jonah, and Matt in the tiny park next to the café.

There's a tall sweetgum tree by the curb. Karl hides behind its wide trunk and spies on his old friends.

They're sipping from pink Shake Shack cups, along with a fourth person Karl doesn't recognize. Matt tosses his cup in a trash can and asks loudly, "Are you ready, String-binis?"

The fourth friend, Karl's replacement, takes out a little video camera, and the Fabulous Flying Stringbinis perform for both passersby and posterity. First comes the Stringbini Handstand: Jonah squats with his hands on the grass in front of him while Lizette and Matt step on his hands with one foot apiece and shout, "Hey!"

Behind his tree trunk, standing in a lake of sweetgum prickly balls, Karl wishes desperately that he could cross the street and join his old friends, even if they do look extremely stupid. He regrets that he ever mocked (even silently, to himself) Jonah's braces and Matt's hyperactivity. It would be so much better to clown around with them than to hide behind a tree, humiliated by a pretty girl who couldn't care less about him.

Here comes the stunt called Falling Down Sideways, which he made up himself. Lizette—a halfhearted String-bini, it seems—stands straight and tall while Jonah and Matt play a drumroll on their thighs. On the count of three, she raises her arms above her head and falls over, straight as a plank. The others catch her just before she hits the ground, shouting, "Hey!" Without Karl there, her weight surprises them; she hits the grass, and sighs.

Thumping music comes from the café next to the park. Cara's date turns out to be the singer of the band that's playing on the small stage. Out in front of the others, he throws his head around as if he were conducting an orchestra with it. Cara smiles like the Mona Lisa.

"Karl Petrofsky, right?"

Huh? Whuh? Who—?

A girl has come up behind him: the weird one from school, with the immobile hair and the plaid slacks that always have a straight crease—the one who drags around a small rolling suitcase instead of a backpack, and therefore looks like a flight attendant as she strides through the halls.

She sticks her hand out straight, to shake his. "Samantha Abrabarba. Nice to meet you. Why are you hiding behind a tree?"

"No reason. I just—didn't have anything to do."

"On a Friday night? Tut, tut. But look on the bright side: that means I can interview you. How about this bench— shall we?"

Samantha, it turns out, wants to profile him for *The Emancipator*, as the quiet genius of the junior class and next year's presumed valedictorian. The prospect of having the whole school read about his prodigious brainpower appeals to him in the same way that large quantities of water appealed to the Wicked Witch of the West—but he doesn't want to walk away, because that would mean losing sight of Cara and the Stringbinis.

He follows her to the yellow bench outside the Enchilada Encantada, the Mexican restaurant, and answers her questions distractedly—about his study habits, and who was his most influential teacher, and what extracurricular activities he's involved in. Hearing that he, um, doesn't do any extracurricular activities, she rests her leather-bound pad on her lap and lectures him. "That's really not smart, you know. Even with grades like yours, colleges want to see that you're, quote, well-rounded, unquote. *Every*body does something. You're not abnormal, are you? Just kidding. I mean, I don't love tutoring dumb, lazy freshmen, but I do it—and working on the newspaper, you wouldn't believe how much crap I have to do, pardon the expression."

Though depressed and a hundred feet away in spirit, Karl can't resist: "You do a lot of crap on the newspaper?"

"I know, you think I'm just a trained dog, doing what I'm supposed to do, when and where I'm supposed to do it. But not everyone has your grades. The rest of us have to find any way we can to shine."

Despite her announced ambition to become a *New York Times* reporter, Samantha talks much more than she listens. When Karl (not wanting to sound like a walking computer in her article) tells about the projects he works on in the garage, like the thermosensitive shingles, she says, "So you're the next Thomas Edison, tinkering in your basement laboratory, pouring chemicals into beakers?"

"No. In the garage. Without beakers."

"But you're planning to go into chemistry, right?"

"Not exactly. I don't really know what I want to do."

"Too bad. I do. I want to interview foreign heads of state, and get them to reveal their secret plans. My strategy is, the pretty face will put them off guard. While they try to impress innocent little me, I'll be digging for classified information."

She does have a pretty face, sort of—angular, sharp-featured, with elegantly elongated eyes—but it's weird to hear someone call herself pretty, and she uses way too much makeup and hair spray, and also she's so oblivious to him, even as she asks him questions, that the main impression she gives is of someone born with a defective social-interaction gene.

"I guess I'll go home now," he says.

"That's rude. I'm not as interesting as your beakers?"

"I'm just tired."

"What if I told you I'm working on a top secret exposé? Can you keep this . . ." She lifts a nonexistent hat and pantomimes putting something under it.

"Excuse me?"

"*Under your hat.* Are you slow?"

"What are you talking about?"

She peers around, left and right—a hokey gesture that he's never seen an actual person perform. "Mr. Klimchock told me not to tell anyone, but I can trust you. I'm trying to catch the cheaters, at school, so I can expose them."

Normally fair-complexioned, Karl feels himself growing paler. "Hm," he says, and then adds, "hm."

"The big question is, Who's Doing It? So far I haven't caught anyone, but I'm on the case."

"That's really interesting. But, I'm sorry, I was up late last night, I have to go."

"Not so fast. Just answer a simple question: have you heard anything?"

"No. I really don't know a thing."

Across the street, his old friends are executing the Quick Pick-Me-Up of Death. Lizette crouches, and Jonah and Matt each put a foot on one of her hands, and then she stands fast and flips them up and away, so that they fly, flailing, up and onto the grass. (No, she doesn't have the strength of Hercules. The trick is to perform the move quickly, before the audience, if there is one, notices the boys springing up with their knees.)

"Hey!" his three friends shout.

"Look at those dorks," Samantha says. "Get a life."

"Well. See you at school."

"I guess I could go ask them what they know. I just hope their nerdiness isn't contagious."

She stands up; Karl grabs her by the wrist and pulls her back down.

"A little aggressive, aren't we?" she says, smirking. "Not so shy after all."

"No—I just wanted to ask: are you keeping your eye on anyone in particular?"

"I have certain suspicions. But I wouldn't want to name any names until I have proof."

"That sounds like the right thing to do."

She does her left-right sneaky peek again, and lowers her voice. "Do you see Cara Nzada, in that window across the street? Doesn't it seem a little *strange* that she gets on the high honor roll every year? What's someone like that doing on the high honor roll? Methinks me smells something rotten in New Jersey, and it's not a chemical factory."

"Appearances can be deceiving."

"Come on, Karl. If it walks like a duck and tastes like a duck."

"But you just said you need proof."

"I'm in English and Spanish with her. I've been sitting behind her, one seat over. It's just a matter of time before I catch her in the act."

In the café window, the rock star is leaning way forward

and singing to Cara. She seems pleased and amused—as if this were her due, as queen.

They have a test on *Moby-Dick* coming up on Monday. He has to warn her.

Unless he doesn't.

In the park, Jonah and Matt are doing the Winter Pepper, the opposite of a somersault. Lizette is staring at Karl.

He turns his head sharply, away from Lizette, away from Samantha.

"I can see it now: 'First High School Student Ever to Win Pulitzer Prize.'"

"But why are you so fixated on this?" Karl asks. "Cheating isn't that big a deal—relatively speaking. It's not the worst thing in the world."

"Are you kidding? This is a sensational story: 'Behind the wholesome suburban facade lurks a festering pit of dishonesty.'"

"A 'festering pit'?"

"Come on, Karl, doesn't it bother you that people like Cara get better grades than everybody else, without even studying? When I catch them, I'm going to print their names in three-inch letters on the front page, with the headline, 'DIE, CHEATERS, DIE.'"

Lizette takes a step toward Karl. Whatever blood was left in his face now drains at high speed.

She doesn't cross the street, though. She calls to the others and leads them away, out of the park, up State Street.

"You know, you're actually a decent conversationalist. Most people are so boring—all they want to talk about is Me Me Me. They're so self-involved. I hate that, don't you?"

He watches his three friends plus his replacement recede into the distance. Sadness nearly smothers him.

"Hey—I just thought of something. You could help me catch the cheaters!"

"I could?"

"You're the guy they'll all come to, to see if you'd give them answers. You're the perfect bait. I bet people have approached you already."

"No, not really."

"Well, it'll happen. And when it does, you'll say, Yes! You can go undercover and catch the whole rotten bunch of them!"

She reaches around and pats herself on the back. "Who's clever? Who's a muckraker? Thank you, thank you."

A police car races past them with its lights flashing, blue, white, and red. The siren gives one startling blast, and Karl jumps off the bench.

"I'd better get going now. See you, bye."

"I'll check in with you, Karl. Very discreetly. We'll make a great team."

She laughs, behind him, a happy little bird.

His mother is reading a book in the living room, with her nightly mug of tea wrapped in one hand. (It's the bright orange jack-o'-lantern mug Karl painted in second grade, faded now, but still her favorite.) Before she can speak even one teasing syllable about his date, she sees the look on his face and censors herself.

For that, he's grateful.

Chapter 8

Monday morning, on line at the Muffin Man's truck, is that Cara, or does she have an identical cousin who's even more attractive?

The hair is shorter, it swoops across the top of her forehead, then plunges down like a curved blade to just under her chin. She's wearing a short black skirt and a red halter top with flowery golden Chinese-style brocade. (Wow.)

The iPod cover, leopard-spotted, answers the question: yep, that's Cara.

Karl hasn't been able to get her out of his mind since Friday night. Ten times he dialed her number minus the last digit. His options basically boil down to these: tell her off and walk away, or ask if she had some good reason for treating him like a small flying insect, the kind you swat without even noticing, and *then* walk away. He can't do either, though, because what if there was some extenuating circumstance? Then his angry accusations will bounce back and splatter him in the face.

She smiles sleepily as she waits her turn, white wires trailing down from her earbuds. He could keep walking and pretend he didn't see her, but that would be so cowardly. Really: Lizette was right, at some point, you have to get a spine.

"Hi," he murmurs, joining her on line.

She nods—to the music, not him—and then shuts it off.

"Morning, Mister Nice Guy."

"You better not be cutting in," growls the slovenly student behind her.

"I'm not buying anything," Karl mumbles.

This isn't a good place to confront Cara, but Karl prods himself. *No excuses.*

"You weren't home Friday night," he says.

"Uh-oh, stalker alert."

"Around seven-thirty, I mean."

"Double alert: stalker with a wristwatch."

Then she remembers.

"Ohhhhhh," she says. "Oops—memory failure." She blinks ironically, impersonating a silent-movie heroine. "Can you ever forgive me?"

"You really just forgot?"

The blinking stops. An evasive smile bends her lips. "No, I didn't forget."

He can't speak the words out loud: *So, you blew me off intentionally?*

"I wanted to hear this band play, and the singer invited

me. But I didn't want to hurt your feelings. I guess I handled the situation poorly, huh?"

There's no point answering.

"But it's over now, it's in the past. We can laugh about it. Ha ha ha ha ha."

Karl doubts he will ever laugh again.

"Come on, don't hide in your Tomb of Gloom. Give me a chance to make it up to you. Tell you what: after school today, I'll go home with you and we'll play Genie and Master. Your wish is my command. Would that pay off my debt to society?"

He stumbles as they step off the curb. The lady inside the Muffin Man truck says, in a thick Russian accent, "Yes, what muffin today?"

Karl has a decision to make: to let go of the humiliation and see what might happen in his room later, or to refuse, because she will treat him like an endlessly abusable puppy for as long as he allows it.

He can't decide, but he holds her books for her as she unwraps her chocolate-chip muffin. They're heading up the winding path to the school's side entrance *(What could I ask for if I'm the Master?)*—when Jon Higginbottom, a dancer with huge shoulders, appears from nowhere, dips Cara in his arms so they look like the *Gone With the Wind* poster, and starts purring to her in pseudo-Italian. *"Mi scatellini, mi pocciabelli, non me sapito, rigatoni, che questo!"*

She laughs as he kisses her pale throat.

"Who is-a this person?" Jon asks, nodding at Karl. "I kill-a heem!"

"No, you mustn't," Cara says, "for he is my long-lost half-brother from Latvia."

From there to the lockers, where he hands over her books, Karl trails just behind them. It's the longest two-hundred-yard walk of his life, but at least it settles the Cara question once and for all.

Not until Samantha Abrabarba pinches his arm at the door-way of Ms. Singh's classroom—where an essay test on *Moby-Dick* will begin just minutes from now—does Karl realize that he forgot to warn Cara about Samantha. It's too late now, but he races down the aisle and snags the seat that's behind Cara and one over, so Samantha can't sit there.

She pounces on the seat next to his, hissing, "Dum-dum, I *told* you that's where I have to sit! Trade with me!"

Stalling until Ms. Singh arrives, Karl pretends to agree, but "accidentally" drops the contents of his backpack on the floor—at least, that's his plan, but there are too many books in the backpack, they're jammed in tight and won't come out. He has already said, "Whoops," and here he is, shaking the upside-down pack while Samantha sneers, "What's your problem?" The moment seems to last a century, as if they'd turned into a diorama at the Museum of Natural History—until Ms. Singh enters the room and three books slide out of the backpack, slapping the floor loudly, one after the other.

Usually, Ms. Singh bounds into the room with a bright, toothy smile, but today she's subdued. Instead of roaming the room and gesticulating from one bell to the next, she takes a seat behind her desk and asks her students to please settle down.

They await a grim personal announcement—*I've been diagnosed with a rare skin condition, and will soon turn into a reptile*—but that's not what they hear.

"I want to talk to you about cheating."

Karl's stomach becomes a clenched fist. How much does she know?

"Apparently, some students, no one knows how many, have been breaking the rules. In case any of you are involved, I just want to spend a minute talking you out of it. I understand, it's hard to preach honesty when you see CEOs on trial all the time on the news. I know it may seem like you *have* to cheat to succeed. But that's not true—and look what happens to them when they're caught. Aside from the fines, and going to prison, they're disgraced. Their names become synonymous with dishonesty. Do you really think they can laugh that off and say, 'Who cares?' I don't. How would you like to go through life knowing that every person who hears your name thinks, *crook*? To me, that sounds like hell on earth. I'm not saying you have to be a saint. I don't claim to be perfect myself—I kept using my student ID for discount tickets long after college—but there are plenty of things I won't do. I won't keep money a cashier gave me by mistake, because it comes out of their pocket at the end of the night. And I never cheated on a test, ever. Seriously. Speaking of which, you all need to remember how high the stakes are, if you get caught cheating. I want you to be honest because you're good people, not because you're terrified that colleges will find out you cheated—but if honor isn't enough, then okay, let's have a moment of silence and think about the consequences before we start the test."

During the ensuing quiet, Karl makes a decision: he wants out of the Confederacy.

The trouble is, Blaine and the others are depending on him.

As if to confirm this, Blaine gives Karl a little raise of the eyebrow, as if to say, *Amazing, isn't it, how these teachers jabber on?*

As for the others, Noah doodles in his notebook, ignoring Ms. Singh altogether; Tim, in his own private time zone, seems to be counting his teeth, touching each one with his fingertip.

"All right, let's get started. Of the four essays I told you to prepare, I'm going to ask you to write number three: 'Even monomaniacal Captain Ahab has more to him than the quest for revenge against Moby-Dick. Referring especially to the chapter entitled "The Symphony," discuss the complexity of Ahab's character. (Hint: Note his symbolic references to greenery and land, as a contrast to the sea.)' I made up this question myself, and I happen to know you can't buy an answer online. Also, you won't be needing your laptops today."

She takes a stack of baby blue test booklets from her desk drawer and hands half of them to Juliette Chang, half to Phillip Upchurch, who hands all but one over to Tim with an expression of severe disgust: looking forward, Karl can tell, to the day when he will no longer have to sit in a classroom full of pathetic losers.

"In case my sermon wasn't convincing," Ms. Singh explains, "I've learned that it's harder for students to cheat when they take tests longhand."

Who would dare to groan, when a groan equals a confession of guilt? She has stopped the Confederates cold, and she doesn't even know it. Karl wrote essays for all four questions and emailed them to the others, but now they have no way to use his work—and, knowing them, they didn't even bother to read what he sent, just copied the text and formatted it so the letters would look white and invisible on their screens, until they turned the words black and paraphrased them during the test. They're on their own now, unprepared. Karl couldn't help them if he wanted to.

An unexpected calamity: they'll all become suspects now, Blaine, Tim, Noah, and Cara, because why would all four of them suddenly flunk a test after getting As all year?

When the blue books arrive, Karl takes one and passes the rest to Samantha, who keeps her ravenous eyes on Cara's back, hungry for a glimpse of wrongdoing that she won't get today.

Or will she?

After writing a paragraph from memory about Ahab's sorrow over his young wife, abandoned a day after the wedding when he returned to sea, Karl glances up at Cara—more in compassion than resentment—and sees something peculiar. As she writes, she keeps flipping up the hem of her short skirt and then flipping it down again.

Oh.

He remembers that day at the food court, centuries ago: *I don't completely trust computers.* An old-fashioned girl.

To his right, Samantha is craning her neck, trying to see around Brett Handshoe's shoulder.

There's nothing on his desk that Karl can drop that would make a noise loud enough to attract Ms. Singh's attention. (Working at the front of the room, she keeps her head down, willfully refusing to hunt for cheaters.) With no other options, he fakes a coughing attack.

Ms. Singh looks up. "Are you all right, Karl?"

Clearing his throat, "Sorry. Yeah. *Cccchhhhmmm.* Thanks."

Noticing Samantha's neck gymnastics—Karl's goal, achieved—Ms. Singh says, "Samantha, please settle down."

The students don't hear that last word, though, because an announcement over the P.A. system drowns her out: "Will Cara Nzada please report to the assistant principal's office? Cara Nzada—to the assistant principal's office. Don't finish your test. Come now, and bring all of your belongings."

The voice is Mr. Klimchock's, and his words go through Karl like a spear. It's almost as if Klimchock were watching them through a hole in the ceiling.

Cara says to Ms. Singh, "So, I guess I'm supposed to go now."

Ms. Singh gives Cara a mournful gaze. "I guess that's right."

Cara drops her purple pen into her black bag. She hands Ms. Singh her test booklet. "Oh well."

Ms. Singh takes the booklet and turns her face away.

Cara gives Karl an amused little pucker of a smile. He has no idea what she finds amusing, or how she can smile.

He's churning inside, and he's not even the one who got caught.

When the door closes behind Cara, Ms. Singh says tensely, "Concentrate on your work, people."

"Karl, what's the matter with you?"

He's passing the band room, where the empty black music stands crowd around randomly like a flock of crows, when Samantha catches up with him, in a huff.

"I *told* you I wanted to sit there. I could have caught her. I could have reported on her in the paper."

"Sorry."

Fortunately, Samantha takes French and he has German next, so he doesn't have to listen to her ranting once the bell rings.

Halfway through the period, window gazing, he sees a girl in a short black skirt escorted into the student parking lot by the security lady. Cara is carrying a lumpy Hefty bag: the contents of her locker, he assumes. She's not smirking any more. She tosses the Hefty bag into the backseat of her grape-colored VW bug, and climbs in. She seems fairly calm, for a person who has just gotten kicked out of school—that is, until she starts the car, and roars out of the lot at highway speed.

They meet at Blaine's convertible. Except for Tim, chomping on an Italian sub with stinky onion slivers hanging down, none of them takes a bite of lunch.

Noah gets straight to the point: "Do you think she gave him our names?"

"Whoa, hold on." That's Blaine, smiling, trying to impose calm on the others. "We don't even know for sure why he called her down."

"Yes we do," Vijay says. "There's only one explanation."

That they would suspect Cara of betraying them all seems unfair to Karl. "She wouldn't give him our names. That's not what she's like."

Noah lets out a snort. "You think she'd really say no if he offered to let her off? Just to protect *us*?"

"Hold on, let's think logically," Ian says. (There's sweat on his forehead—a first.) "If she gave him our names, why would he send her home with all her stuff? He wouldn't."

"Could be a cover-up," Vijay says. "So we'll think we're safe, while he collects evidence against us."

Tim talks with his mouth full. "Wow, that's so paranoid."

"Maybe he sent her home to think over his offer," Blaine suggests. "Maybe he said, 'You have two choices: tell me their names, or forget about college. Take a day to make your decision.'"

Ian agrees. "That sounds like his style."

Vijay has more sweat on his face than Ian. "We have to talk to her. If she hasn't already told him everything, we have to get to her before she does."

Noah shakes his head miserably. "I don't see what we can say. What would convince her to act against her own self-interest?"

Karl reminds him: "How about, *You go down alone*?"

Blaine shakes his head. "That's great in the abstract, but not if Klimchock has her by the throat."

"There's really only one way to convince her to keep quiet," Ian says.

"There is?" Tim perks up. "I didn't think there was *any.*"

They all look to Ian for their salvation. Before he can speak, though, Karl spots Samantha at the school's back door, surveying the parking lot with a flat hand shading her eyes. He dives down behind Blaine's BMW: an instinctive reflex, but also heroic, in that he's saving the entire Confederacy from her scrutiny.

"What's up, Karl? You're not going to throw up on my car, are you?"

"Ssh! Don't say my name!" He stays down, crouching. "That girl at the door—don't look at her!—is she coming this way?"

"No, she's going back inside. Who is she, your ex-wife?"

Karl peeks over the hood before standing.

"She's hunting for cheaters so she can put their names in the school newspaper."

A spontaneous moment of silence . . . then Noah croaks a string of four-letter words.

"One crisis at a time," Blaine says. "Ian, what's your plan? How do we keep Cara from giving Klimchock our names?"

"We have to threaten her."

"No!" Karl blurts. "That's ridiculous!"

"It's better than getting kicked out of school."

"We wouldn't have to threaten anything really awful," Blaine muses. "Just enough so she'd rather not talk."

No one has any suggestions to offer. And no one is volunteering to make the call. Maybe the odious suggestion will sink into the earth and be forgotten.

"We don't have to call her," Vijay says. "We could send an anonymous email."

"You can do that?" Noah asks. "How?"

"It's not hard. I can set the Reply To and From headers to any name we choose. It's called spoofing an address."

"I know what to put in the email," Ian says grimly. "Start spoofing, Veej."

"No!" Karl protests. "This is crazy!"

"Matter of life and death, Buds." Blaine lays a hand on Karl's shoulder. "She's not exactly the most reliable person in the world. You must have figured that out by now."

Karl steps back, away from Blaine's hand. "I don't care. We shouldn't do this."

But Vijay already has his laptop open, he's tapping away, and here comes Ian to type the message.

A few moments from now Karl will wish he'd taken Vijay's laptop, thrown it on the blacktop, and stomped on it—but that's hindsight. At the crucial instant he just watches with his mouth agape as Ian types, DON'T GIVE HIM ANY NAMES OR WE'LL DESTROY YOUR CAT.

"Are you out of your mind?" Karl shouts.

Vijay clicks the Send button.

"It's a desperate situation," Ian says.

"You're going to kill her cat?!"

"I didn't say anything about a cat."

"You did, you said you'd destroy her cat."

"I said we'd destroy her *car*."

"No you didn't—you said CAT."

Vijay opens his Sent Messages box. There's the proof.

Ian stares down at the keyboard. "The *r* is right next to the *t*," he mumbles.

"Should we send a correction?" Vijay asks the group.

"Wait a minute," Noah says. "Does she have a cat?"

Karl and Blaine answer in unison, "Yes."

"Well, it's okay, then," Noah says. "It'll work either way."

In grievous turmoil, Karl stalks away, hating them, wanting never to see them again. He ignores Blaine, who's calling his name, and goes back inside the school.

Then he remembers that his lunch is sitting on the hood of Blaine's car.

Too bad. Consider it lost.

In spite of the way she stood him up so her singer friend could serenade her, Karl heads straight to Cara's apartment after school—at a trot for most of the way, in case the Confederates decide to bully her in person.

She's still wearing the same outfit she had on this morning—the short black skirt, the red and gold halter top—even though that seems like a lifetime ago. Her eye makeup is unsmeared; she hasn't been crying.

It's almost as if the whole day never happened . . . until she speaks. "Who are you, the Cat Destroyer?"

"I tried to stop them but they wouldn't listen. They panicked."

"Wimps."

"They didn't mean to threaten your cat, by the way. That was a typo."

"What do they really want to destroy? My hat?"

"Your car. But they didn't mean it."

She goes down the narrow hall to her room. He follows, hoping that's okay.

Lying on her side on the bed, she plays with the cat, who lets her roll him back and forth, oblivious to the death threat. Karl has never seen a sloppier room: she's got dirty laundry on the floor, a half-eaten cookie on a tissue on the dresser, CDs strewn all over the place, and a chaotic sea of necklaces on the table that serves as her desk, along with a flotilla of makeup.

She wags the cat's outstretched arm. "They really thought I would give Klimchock their names? What idiots. I guess they assumed I'm just like them."

There are red, yellow, and blue knobs on Cara's dresser: a leftover trace of childhood. At the opposite extreme, she also has half a dozen posters of guys taped to the walls— rippling chests, facial stubble, mirrored sunglasses. One of them is flying upside down with crossed skis. If Karl had seen this room sooner, he could have saved himself a lot of false hopes.

"So—are you okay?" he asks.

"I'm fine."

"What did he say to you?"

"Basically, he said, 'Give me all of your friends' names or you're permanently expelled.' So, that's that. Free at last."

"He really expelled you?"

"He said I'm free to sue the school district, and he looks forward to it, because that would attract huge publicity and might inspire a zero tolerance movement nationwide."

She jiggles the cat's furry white belly. Her calm amazes him. If this happened to him, he would probably be weeping right now.

On the folding table with her necklaces and makeup, there's a picture of a man in an Indiana Jones hat. He's got a bushy mustache, a black shirt and yellow tie under a striped jacket, and a joking sort of sinister look. The picture looks like an album cover from the 1960s or 1970s; he's almost definitely a musician, the type who totally disdains mainstream people.

"Is that your father?" Karl asks.

She strokes the cat's head. The purring sounds like snoring. "Yup."

"Is he still alive?"

"Hope so. We haven't heard from him in a long time."

To Karl, that seems just as bad as getting expelled.

"I wish I could do something to help," he says. "About school, I mean."

"I don't need help. It's a relief, to be done with that stinkin' hole."

"What about your mother? She's not going to be happy."

"She's not going to know. I can get to the mail first—since I'll be home all day."

He doubts she's right. Sooner or later, her mother will find out.

"I'm done with them," he announces. "Just for your information. I'm not going to help them cheat anymore."

"That's your business, not mine."

Disappointing: he thought she'd at least appreciate the gesture.

"Look, Karl. We're extremely different people, in case you hadn't noticed. We might as well get real."

Since he has nothing to lose, he says what he really thinks. "You're so smart. You could do anything you wanted. You don't have to break the rules every minute of the day. It looks like you're *trying* to get in trouble."

She stands up; the cat leaps away. She puts a CD in the boom box on her dresser and turns it on, loud. He doesn't recognize the song: voice like a buzz saw, drummer smashing the cymbals over and over, fast. Without answering him, Cara nods her head to the music, keeping her back to him.

"I guess I'll go," he says.

She doesn't stop him.

Halfway down the stairs, he realizes that the purpose of his visit got lost somewhere along the way. He came here to offer comfort and friendship in her time of trouble—but somehow that didn't happen.

RULE #9: If you start cheating, don't even think about stopping. When your grades suddenly go into free fall, what will your teachers think? Maybe I should have called this Rule #1: Don't start cheating unless you plan to keep it up. If anyone out there wishes I'd shared that little tidbit up front, all I can say is, Go ahead, sue me.

Chapter 9

Karl has been searching for Blaine all day long, so he can officially quit the Confederacy. But Blaine is nowhere to be seen. Vijay explains why: today was the regional Model U.N. conference. Karl's announcement will have to wait.

Memories of Lizette distract him all through his last period. That second day of school, when she came up to him and Jonah and Matt at their cafeteria table and asked if she could eat with them—that must have been hard for her to do. But she got past the nervous introductions, and after a while Jonah and Matt calmed down (a girl! at their table!) and they went back to talking about how you could play baseball in the snow if you had a black ball, and then Lizette said, in her swampiest Florida accent, "Y'all talk like a bunch of Yankees," and they didn't know if she was serious or kidding until she snickered (under her cap's visor), and the sight of her front teeth peeking impishly over her lower lip marked the beginning of Karl's early crush . . . the best part of which, for Karl, was that she laughed at his jokes, like at the assembly where Klimchock announced the removal of all vending machines for health reasons, Karl whispered, "His real name is Mr. Tater—first name Dick," and Lizette let out such a loud hiccup of a laugh that she got sent to the office.

The way she used to look at him sometimes, with that mischievous, sealed-lip grin, it really seemed as if she liked him the other way. But then she would punch him in the arm and call him Donkey Head, and yell at him for missing the ball when they played Footnis. And there was that time when they saw Beanie Markowsky refereeing a kids' soccer game in the park, and Lizette sighed and said, "She's so graceful." There was just no way to figure her out.

He's leaving the building as he thinks this—and there, across the street, is Blaine: still in jacket and tie from the Model U.N., leaning against his car in the shade of a locust tree, talking to the cheerleader Nikki Tunis, who's bathing him in beams of adoration. Blaine seems to be enjoying the worship and gives her arm a friendly squeeze, which encourages Nikki to bring her face even closer to his.

Karl approaches them; Nikki rolls her eyes at the intrusion. "Can I talk to you?" he asks Blaine.

"Is it a quickie?"

"No, probably not."

Blaine sighs and tells Nikki he'll call her tonight. She gives him a coy, promise-filled smile (for Karl, there's a wrinkled nose) and departs with an unnaturally straight back and an oscillating behind.

"Karl, if you weren't the most important man in my life, I'd pound your head into the ground. Come on, I'll give you a ride home."

In the convertible, Karl lets Blaine report on his day. "The representative from Myanmar was cute. When I said her country could overthrow their military dictatorship just like mine did, she said, 'Good golly, Mister Mali!'"

Karl can see why that might be funny under other circumstances. But now it's his turn to talk, and for some reason, he's having a hard time breathing. "I wanted to tell you—I decided to quit. I'm not going to help you guys anymore."

Blaine drives with his right hand on top of the wheel, casually. If he's experiencing panic, he keeps it hidden. "Just one problem, amigo. You can't run out on us. A lot of people are depending on you."

"Not a lot, not really. Only a few."

"What I meant was, *we're* counting on you. Your friends. Me, Vijay, Ian, Noah. And Tiny Tim, too. We've got a lot at stake."

"I don't want to do it anymore. I'm done."

Mr. Cool isn't taking this too seriously. "Karl, not too many people in this world can say that they single-handedly got their friends into good colleges. You're our hero. And heroes don't bail on their buddies. Right?"

"I *hate* doing this."

"Don't you remember the reason you started helping us in the first place? Just because Cara's gone, that doesn't change the big picture—Klimchock's still evil. He hasn't gone humane all of a sudden."

"I don't *want* to help you, after the way you treated her."

For once, Blaine can't find an easy comeback. He nods as he drives, searching for an answer.

During the silence, certain details come into sharp focus for Karl: the stainless perfection of the beige leather seats, the dustlessness of the charcoal gray dash. (Does he have a cleaning service come in once a week?) Then there's the driver himself, with never a hair out of place nor a bulge in any pocket. On Karl's own jeans, meanwhile, the thighs have worn thin and lost most of their blueness, and his key ring has nearly eaten a hole in the pocket. Shabby, shabby, shabby.

"You would never have talked to me except for wanting my help," he says.

"I'm not so sure about that."

"I am."

"Don't be. There's more to this than meets the eye. See, my mother has been telling me, my whole life, 'Certain people can be useful to you, and you should cultivate them as friends.' I always thought she was kind of insidious—but now I see it differently. Let's say, someday, you're Bill Gates and I'm the CEO of Shore Investments. It's not that I *need* you, I'm doing just fine on my own. But wouldn't it be cool if we were old high school buddies and I could call you up and say, 'Billy, you old digital dog, what's up? Feel like investing a few million in Romanian salt mines today?' You're going to do really well in life, Karl. I like the idea of being your amigo from high school."

Here's one way to measure Blaine's charm: he has just admitted that he wants to exploit Karl someday, and how does Karl react? His insides are all warm and tickly, he loves Blaine like a brother.

As they pull up behind the unfamiliar white Volvo in front of Karl's house, Blaine says, "So what do you think? Can we keep our successful partnership—"

"Hey!" Karl shouts, rudely interrupting—because, inside his garage, Samantha Abrabarba has pulled the sheet off his project, and she's running her hand over the slick stainless steel dome, which shines blindingly as the afternoon sun angles in.

"Karl?" Blaine asks. "Why are you building a giant metal tortoise?"

Karl runs out of the car, grabs the sheet, and draws it over the shining dome.

"Very interesting," Samantha says. She's all in white today, slacks, blouse, and belt: a fashion statement in a language Karl doesn't understand. "So smooth and tightly welded. Does it fly?"

"You can't come in here and poke around in my stuff. That's trespassing!"

"No it's not. I'm your friend. Only strangers can trespass."

Is that true? The confusion delays him for a moment—but only for a moment. "You shouldn't be in here. You have to leave."

"Why? Is it a surprise for me?"

It sounds just like something Cara would say, teasingly. But Samantha is serious.

"Maybe. I'm not sure. Depends on how it turns out."

"That would be so amazing, if you dedicated an invention to me!"

Blaine has followed Karl in. He's smirking.

"Hey, Karl. I'm not interrupting anything, am I?"

Samantha studies Blaine as if he were a museum exhibit. "You're a friend of Karl's?"

"You look surprised."

"Karl doesn't seem like he would have a friend who stepped out of *GQ*."

"Actually, we make a good pair, Karl and me. *GQ* and IQ."

Putting Samantha and Blaine together in the same room (or garage) is like tossing lit matches around at an oil refinery. The faster Karl can get rid of her, the better.

"I'm kind of busy," he tells Samantha. "Could I call you later?"

"You could if you had my phone number, but you still haven't asked for it."

"Could you write it down for me?" he asks, blushing because of the audience.

"My things are in the car. Got a pen and paper?"

He tears a flap off the top of an empty carton and digs an old carpenter's pencil out of his father's never-used toolbox. The pencil wears a coating of fine gray grime.

As she writes, she asks, "Have you two been friends a long time? Or is this something recent? Something sudden?"

She winks at Karl, but he refuses to receive the signal.

"We grew up together," he says. "Cub Scouts."

"Hm." Samantha hands Karl her phone number, written in large, bold numbers. "On a different subject—does either of you know how to reach Cara Nzada? I can't find her address or phone number anywhere."

GQ and IQ zip their lips.

"One of you has to have it. You've spent enough time hovering around her."

"Why do you want to talk to her?" Karl asks.

She gives him an exasperated scowl, as in, *Are you totally stupid? This is a secret investigation, remember?* "No particular reason. Just to chat."

Karl imagines Samantha grilling Cara in her apartment. *Who helped you cheat? You might as well tell me, I'll find out anyway.*

"Sorry," he says, "I don't know how to reach her."

Blaine, incredibly, shows no anxiety whatsoever. "She just moved. She hasn't given me her new info yet. Guess she didn't give it to you either, huh, Karl?"

"No, she didn't."

"How about the old 'info,' then? There's probably a recording on the line."

"Nope. I tried. It just says the number's been disconnected. Sorry."

"Seems like you two would rather not have me talk to her." Samantha wags the dirty pencil at Karl. "What does Cara know about you that you don't want anybody finding out?"

Blaine guffaws. Following his lead, Karl chuckles.

"Okay," Blaine says, "you nailed us. We're smuggling ice cubes out of Canada. Too bad, now you know too much, we can't let you live."

"You're so useless." Samantha sighs. She taps the piece of cardboard in Karl's hand. "Call me tonight. We can talk about your new friends. Don't be shy—I'll be waiting, Karl."

She hands him back the pencil and walks out to the white Volvo with a weirdly jaunty stride.

"Lover boy," Blaine says as Samantha's car swings around in the cul-de-sac.

"I didn't do anything to encourage her."

"You don't have to. You've got that brainy charisma thing going on."

Alone with Blaine again, Karl remembers what they were saying before Samantha interrupted. Having to say no to Blaine is like wearing a lead cape over his shoulders. He wishes he could erase everything from the moment he joined the Confederacy until now.

"Just so I can sleep tonight—you're not going to tell Flight Attendant Barbie our secrets, are you?"

Karl scowls at him, offended.

"Sorry. I just had to make sure."

"Why don't you think about stopping, Blaine? Instead of trying to change my mind, why don't you change yours? Before Samantha catches you."

"I'd like to make you happy, Karl—but your cult of honesty is too weird for me. Besides, I can't stop, or my grades would drop off the edge of the world. The teachers would send me to the guidance counselor, and she'd ask if there's any trouble at home, and then she'd call my parents. It's like dominos—one false move and everything collapses."

Karl straightens his spine—*Stand up to him*, he tells himself—and discovers that he's an inch taller than Blaine.

"I'm not going to help you anymore," he says. "If you want to be my friend, you have to respect my decision."

Blaine's calm turns out to be a mere shell. Through it bursts a thunderbolt of panic. "You're screwing us!"

The explosion means that Karl has finally broken free—or so he thinks. Exhilarated, he plans his future: as soon as Blaine leaves, he'll call Lizette.

"You're forcing me to go a way I really don't want to go," Blaine says, shaking his head mournfully.

Karl reads this as a bluff and stands firm.

Blaine opens his cell phone and speed-dials.

"Who are you calling?"

Blaine exhales grimly, as if deeply regretting the piano he's about to drop on Karl's head. So far, it still looks like a fake-out.

"Hi, it's Blaine. Listen, I'm with Karl, at his house, and he says he refuses to help us anymore. I tried to change his mind, but he won't listen. What do you want me to do? . . . I've tried, believe me. . . . Okay, but how, exactly?" A look of alarm. An uncomfortable glance at Karl. "You're sure you want me to do that?" He turns his back to Karl. "But— No, but— No, I don't. Okay, all right, I understand. . . . I'll tell him. . . . Bye."

If not for the buzzing voice on the other end, Karl wouldn't have believed this: somewhere out there, a mysterious Mr. Big controls Blaine like a puppet.

"Who was that?" he asks.

"Can't tell you."

"What's the message you're supposed to deliver?"

"I'm sorry about this, Karl. You know I like you."

"Stop saying you like me."

"This isn't how I prefer to deal with people."

Karl gives him an impatient glare.

"Okay, here's what he said. You can't quit now, or someone will set your old friends up so it looks like they cheated, and report them to Klimchock."

"What old friends do you mean?"

"You know. Jonah. Matt. Lizette."

It's weird to hear these syllables from Blaine's lips—kind of like Zeus addressing a humble shepherd by name. *Yo, Woolius.* You don't expect them to be paying attention up on Mount Olympus.

"Who was that on the phone?"

"I can't say. You don't even know him. But he knows you."

"Sounds like another bluff to me. Remember *We'll destroy your cat?*"

"Believe me, Karl, this guy doesn't make false threats. You don't want to test him." Blaine backs out of the garage. "Don't shoot the messenger, okay?"

How will Karl take this setback? Depression would be understandable. Despair, definitely. But his spirit has grown over the past weeks, and what he's feeling right now, more than anything, is anger. He's so mad, in fact, that when he heads back into the house, he flings open the door at the back of the garage, fast; his windbreaker flaps in the breeze, and the doorknob gets caught on the windbreaker's pocket. This hardly seems possible, but (Petrofsky's Second Law of Klutzodynamics: When you're most agitated, that's when you do the most ridiculously clumsy things) the knob wedges itself into the small pocket inside the outer pocket, and when Karl tries to free himself, he can't. His anger turns to frantic frustration. He can either stay hooked indefinitely, or he can rip the windbreaker to shreds. He's leaning toward the latter.

We'll leave him in this absurd predicament and hope he realizes in time that there's a third, more sensible option: slip the windbreaker off and come back to it later, when he's calmer.

(Remember this the next time you find yourself speared like a hot dog on the two sharp prongs of a dilemma: there's usually a third solution that doesn't involve the destruction of self or property. To find it, take a deep breath, calm down, and *think.*)

Chapter 10

Happy birthday, Karl.

You're seventeen today—old enough to drive alone in your home state, once you pass the road test.

Your friends Vijay and Noah have purchased a special gift for you, a little gizmo that you're sure to love. Go ahead, open it. (Don't look so grim! It's your birthday, for goodness' sake!)

"Oh—it's a pen."

I-BALL, say the letters on the clip. For a few happy milliseconds, he mistakes this for an ordinary pen, a dull but appreciated gift from two guys who cared enough to acknowledge his birthday.

"Click it," Vijay tells him, grinning.

He does.

"Noah, what time is it?" Vijay asks.

"I can't tell. Karl, what does my watch say?"

Karl glances at Noah's watch and sees—huh?—a jittery image of a sneaker on concrete. *His* sneaker. Wait—the image moves—now a silver PT Cruiser is driving by on Noah's watch dial—just like the one that's turning the corner onto Shlink Street.

Vijay moves the tip of the pen so it points at himself, and there he is on the watch dial, crisp and clear. He points it back at the school, and there's Lincoln High, tiny on the dial. "We all chipped in. It's from an online spy store."

"Best birthday present you ever got, right?"

Uncharacteristically peppy, Vijay puts on some unidentifiable accent (Arnold Schwarzenegger?) and says, "It is the maximum in miniaturization."

If they perceive his misery, they don't show it. He'd really like to snap the pen in two and throw the pieces over the nearest roof, but that would be rude, and besides, he's pretty sure they'll be expecting him to use the pen during tomorrow's German test. Which he can't refuse to do, no matter what, or innocent victims will suffer.

Vijay has to get a haircut, and the barbershop is halfway to Karl's house, so they walk together. "We're lucky to live in the electronic age," Vijay remarks.

Deep in his sorrow, Karl blurts a blunt question. "Why do you keep cheating? At some point your luck's going to run out. You'll ruin your life when you didn't need to."

Vijay swings his book bag merrily. "You must be on some kind of antihappiness drug. Lighten up!"

Though he didn't expect to convince Vijay instantaneously, this disappoints Karl.

"You know why I really do it?" Vijay says. "The technical challenge is only half the reason. I like that people need my skill. No one else at school can do this—just me. I wouldn't give that up."

Here's what hurts: Karl *likes* Vijay (though the memory of the cat-destruction threat hangs behind his friendly feelings like a toxic cloud). He really wants to alter Vijay's trajectory before he flies right into Klimchock's wide-open jaws. But he doesn't know how.

"Anyway," Vijay adds, "what's the point of having technology if you don't use it?"

They've come to the barbershop. Vijay shakes Karl's hand and repeats his Happy Birthday wish before going in. Then he reminds Karl to take good care of his gift until tomorrow.

Musings of a young American walking home alone on his seventeenth birthday:

I'm an idiot. All this time, I thought my problem was being too smart, and everyone thinking I'm a geek. But I was wrong—my real problem is, I was too stupid to see through their flattery. And I deserted my real friends. I made every possible mistake.

After a quick stop at home to drop off his backpack, it's over to the driving school on Hillside Avenue—where Jonah is standing at the curb, waiting for his lesson.

He had to trade days because of an orthodontist appointment, he explains. In the awkward minutes before their instructors take them out, they stand together, shifting their weight from foot to foot.

"So—happy birthday," Jonah says. "You going to do anything?"

"No, just going out to eat with my parents."

Karl assumes Jonah must be thinking about the same thing *he's* thinking about: Lizette's birthday, in December, when they went bowling and Matt's fingers got stuck in the ball and he slipped on the slick lane and went sliding halfway to the pins, and they couldn't stop laughing.

But that's not what Jonah's thinking. "How come you dumped us, Karl?" he asks.

Somewhere, a woodpecker drums against a tree trunk. And again.

"I didn't think you were that kind of person—who'd ditch your friends because you found some cooler ones."

"That's not what happened. Really—it's not."

At least, it's only half the story.

"Okay, then, what happened?"

Here comes Mr. Pizzuti, in the blue Corolla, holding his cigarette out the window.

"Lizette got mad at me. We had a fight."

"About what?"

"I can't tell you. But she was right and I was wrong."

Jonah has a habit of covering his braces with his lips at all times, except when he's so happy that he forgets about them. The sun glints brightly now on the steel bonded to his front teeth. "Maybe if I told her you said that, you guys could talk it over and make up."

Make up. As if they were a couple.

"I wish we could, but she won't. It's complicated."

"You never know until you try."

"Usually that's true, but not this time."

During his lesson, Karl imagines Jonah reporting his words to Lizette (*He says he was wrong and you were right!*) and Lizette coming over to ask if he's going to stop cheating now, and him saying he can't, they're blackmailing him, and her not believing him and slapping his face—right cheek, left cheek, right cheek, left cheek—before stomping out and slamming the door. Fortunately, these visions don't interfere with his driving, except for when he fails to stop for a school bus letting off its tiny passengers. (Mr. Pizzuti jams on *his* brake, and the bus driver gives Karl the sort of glower usually reserved for swindlers of widows and orphans.)

His parents take him out to dinner at Beau Thai. After this long, gruesome day, spending his birthday night with his parents is an almost unbearable sorrow. "What would you like to do after dinner, Karl?" his mom asks. "We're up for just about anything."

"Skiing may be hard to arrange this time of year," his dad comments.

"No, um, I made plans with some friends, if that's okay," he lies.

"Oh, the heartbreak," Dad says, pretending to sob.

"Do you want us to drop you off at someone's house?"

"No, it's not till later. I can walk."

At home, he waits in hope and dread for Lizette to call. The phone rings—but it's Grandma Agnes, calling from California to sing "Happy Birthday to You" with her pals at the pool.

Walking to his, er, friend's house—in other words, walking aimlessly through town, on quiet streets where no one will see him—Karl thinks back to other birthdays. There was the party at the tae kwon do place in kindergarten, when Jonah threw up. The blur of parties in the house when he was tiny, recorded in never-watched videos and in the family photo album. (Chocolate all over his face and hands, cone-hat on his head.) The backyard carnival party with the tug-of-war and the egg race.

This birthday stands alone, though. The absolute low point.

The next morning, Karl uses the I-Ball pen to give Tim and Ian the answers to a German test on adjective endings. As he's filling in the -er after gut- (*Ich bin ein guter Student*), the hiss of the P.A. system forewarns everyone that an announcement is coming.

"Karl Petrofsky. Pack your books. You're going to Mr. Klimchock's office. Leave your test where it is. See you soon."

Karl and Herr Franklin stare at each other, equally helpless, equally paralyzed.

"Right now, Karl," says The Voice. "I'm waiting."

Herr Franklin clearly wants to offer support as Karl goes out, but all he can do is place his hand on Karl's shoulder— a hand that burns, partly because Karl knows he doesn't deserve the sympathy, and partly because it's really hot.

The picture in Karl's mind, as he makes the long journey down to the office, comes from *War of the Worlds*, with Tom Cruise: a giant robot tentacle reaches down, grabs a plump, juicy human, and hoists him into the spidery alien vessel, screaming and fighting. Karl's face has gone bloodless. The empty, echoey stairwells still smell like paint. *How did he know? Did someone tell him about the pen? It couldn't have been Herr Franklin.* Past the small display case of trophies won by the math and chess teams, past the exhibition of blue, multiarmed deities painted by Sita Tiwari—*Is there any chance this isn't about cheating?*

At last he arrives at the office, where Mrs. D'Souza, Mr. Klimchock's secretary, keeps a plate of gingerbread cookies on the corner of her desk, a consolation for any student unfortunate enough to be called down to see her boss.

"Mr. Klimchock wanted to see me," Karl mumbles.

"Yes, Karl, I heard. Would you like a cookie first?"

"No, but thanks."

"Good luck."

She does an odd thing with her face. She pulls her lips in tight, knits her brow as if in anguish, and nods. *Courage. Be strong.*

She's a nice person, Karl reflects as he steps through the door. *How can she stand to work for him?*

Mr. Klimchock, sucking on something, holds an open tin of lemon Altoids out to Karl, across his desk. Karl shakes his head, then adds, "No thank you."

"Sit down, sit down," he's told as the assistant principal rises to his feet.

A peculiar calm settles on Karl as he takes a seat. Most likely it's a physiological response to anxiety-overload—but he's actually relieved to be here. No matter what happens, he has escaped once and for all from the Confederacy.

Klimchock moves around the office like a boxer, never

settling in one spot for long. "Expelled? Disgraced? A brilliant career flushed down the toilet? There's no way a boy like you is going to let it happen."

He sounds cheerful. Karl waits for the sledgehammer's blow.

"The good news is, I'm willing to keep this entire incident out of your records."

In his fear of being asked to name names, Karl forgot that part—the penalty for cheating, the permanent record of his crime. He commands himself to hold it together, to stay strong and not think about his parents and their ivy-covered dreams, at least until he's out of here—but his head keeps getting lighter and lighter.

Or, what if . . .

Having nothing to lose, he goes for the long shot. "Um— what are you talking about?"

Klimchock comes up alongside him. Before Karl knows what's happening, Klimchock has snatched the I-Ball pen from his shirt pocket. The assistant principal studies the pen until he finds the tiny lens near the tip. "Denial won't work, Karl. You shouldn't have been so obvious—moving the pen over the paper like a flashlight, *tsk tsk*."

He hands Karl a yellow pad. "I'll keep this pen as evidence. You can use one of mine." Giving Karl a Bic pen from the mug on his desk, he puts a finger to his own lips and says, "I won't say a word. Just write what I need to know and you can leave. No harm, no foul."

Karl rests his hand on the pen so it won't roll away and fall on the floor. He's thinking hard. What could he do that would make a college overlook the note on his records? What he comes up with is: single-handedly rescuing a dozen girls and a nun from a stranded cable car over a rocky gorge.

"Feel free to give me the names any way you like. You can paint them on my wall if that'll make you happy."

When Karl fails to join in Klimchock's chuckle, the assistant principal drums his fingertips on Karl's shoulder. "I know this isn't easy. There are so many nasty names for people who do this. Rat. Stool pigeon. Informer. But there's another way to look at it. When you inform on bad people, you're really a hero. Not a snitch—a whistle-blower. Someone who sees rottenness and reports it, for the common good. What a service you'll be doing for this school! Remember what the Munchkins sang to Dorothy? 'You will be a bust, be a bust, be a bust, in the Hall of Fame.'"

Karl worries that, by stubbornly refusing to take up the pen, he's behaving rudely. The assistant principal checks his watch and paces the room. "I have a little time problem, Karl. I'm supposed to meet with the superintendent in ten minutes. I'm sorry, but I really don't have the luxury of letting you wallow in your qualms. I expect you to do the right thing and save your hide—so let's cut the bull and get down to it."

Karl considers his options. One: sacrifice his future to protect a bunch of slimeballs. Two: turn them in like a cowardly, treacherous sleaze, just to protect himself.

A gentle rap at the door interrupts the stillness. "What is it?" Mr. Klimchock barks.

The door opens slightly, and a small, gift-wrapped box appears, in the palm of a pale hand that belongs, it turns out, to Miss Verp.

"I saw something at Town Stationery and I thought you would—"

Finding Karl there, twisting his neck to see her, Miss Verp freezes with her jaws open.

"Didn't Edna tell you I had a student with me?"

"She stepped away."

"Just leave it on the file cabinet. Go, thanks, good-bye."

The door closes. The mystery gift, in blue and gold metallic wrapping paper, sits cheerily on the gray steel.

"Getting back to business," Klimchock says, "think of it this way. Would your so-called friends risk anything to keep *your* name secret? Would they risk, say, dessert for a month?"

"Cara did," Karl croaks.

"Cara Nzada? You can't compare yourself with her. She has a pathological attitude problem. She'll go far—from misdemeanor to felony to life in a trailer park, looking older than her years."

Until now, Karl wasn't sure he'd be able to withstand the assistant principal's threats. Thanks to this reminder of Klimchock's cruelty, however, Karl discovers that he's stronger than he thought.

"Time's running out. Let's get that hand moving."

Staring at the shiny pink head, Karl can't stop hearing the words *Come to the Dark Side, Luke.*

"You're not going to sacrifice your future for a bunch of brats who used you like a vending machine: put in ten cents' worth of flattery, make the twerp feel like he's in with the in crowd, and out come the right answers. What a bargain."

Ouch.

The eye of the hurricane passes. All is still for a few moments. Klimchock stares out the window, then wanders over to his *Fiddler on the Roof* poster. Turning his back to Karl, he inspects the shoe that rests on the tiny, sagging house. "You may be thinking to yourself, *How did this man get to be so fanatical, so obsessed? Am I right?"*

"Not exactly."

"There's a reason, Karl. If I despise cheating, if rooting it out is my passion, I have good cause. A long time ago, when I was roughly your age, attending this high school, I lost out on something I wanted very badly. And the reason I lost was that the other guy cheated. So—now you're thinking, *Get over it!* But I never did get over it—because it changed the course of my life. It crept into my guts and stayed there. There is nothing on earth I hate more than a cheater."

"What did you lose out on?"

"None of your business. I'm just explaining that I'm not an evil madman who lives to torment teenagers. I seek justice."

Karl does his best to meet Mr. Klimchock's gaze, but his eyes keep drifting away, to the place on the assistant principal's scalp where the creased forehead meets the smooth dome—the swooping line behind which his hair once grew. The startling idea of Klimchock with a full head of hair reminds Karl that the assistant principal was young once, a teenager, and maybe not a vicious maniac. Like a curved universe, this is a concept that's easy to state but hard to grasp. Karl understands this much, though: if an innocent baby can grow up and become Mr. Klimchock, then there's no guarantee that some hideous trauma won't warp *him*, too.

"I'd like to send you back to class now," Mr. Klimchock says, and taps the yellow pad.

Time and fate are closing in on him.

"It's all right, son. I know they manipulated you—I know you didn't do it to improve your own grades. You're not the one I'm after."

He will pay for this the rest of his life if he keeps resisting—all to protect some honorless thieves who (Klimchock has this much right) never cared about him in the slightest—who blackmailed him and threatened his friends to keep him from quitting. (Who *was* that on the phone with Blaine? The question plagues him like an itch he can't reach.)

"It takes strength to separate yourself from your peers," Klimchock says. "But I believe you have what it takes."

What was it Lizette said on his front steps? *Look yourself in the eye and be honest.*

Good advice, but it doesn't seem to apply here.

"Pick up the pen, Karl. Time's running out."

"Sorry. I can't."

Klimchock slaps the *Fiddler on the Roof* poster with a flat hand, so hard that particles of ceiling plaster drift down on them. A wormlike vein has popped up on his forehead. Uck.

"All right. There's one other way. If you can't bring yourself to tell me their names, you can let them hang themselves. You'll cheat one more time, on the next test. I've suspected for a while that you people were sending each other answers via radio signal. I'm right, am I not?"

Karl sees no point in lying. "Mm-hm."

"Fantastic! Because I've ordered a system that will let me see who's receiving your signal. I'll have them dead to rights. You didn't sell them out—they gave themselves away. But, if you warn them, and no one picks up the signal, then I'll know you tipped them off, and it'll be Bye-Bye, Karly."

The next test, though, would be . . . the SAT.

"You don't mean the SAT, right?"

Klimchock considers that for a moment, then smiles contentedly. "Why not? It's perfect—the widest net, to catch the most fish."

Karl can't stretch his brain around this.

"You seem perplexed."

"I just—you can't do this. Not on the SAT."

"I can't?"

If Klimchock is so far beyond the gravitational force of sanity that he doesn't understand, then nothing Karl can say will bring him back down to earth.

"Remember the goal, Karl. Sometimes justice requires extreme measures."

Even if Karl were willing to lure what remains of the Confederacy into Klimchock's net—which he's not—he would never do it on the SAT. That would be like . . . like . . . spray painting his name, address, and Social Security number all over police headquarters. This isn't some trivial little grammar quiz—Klimchock is messing around with the Educational Testing Service!

"I wonder," the assistant principal says, "if we've been wrong about you all this time."

"What do you mean?"

"We all assumed your grades were real. Maybe they're not. Maybe you've been cheating since grammar school. Is that how you always get everything right?"

"No—I just started a few weeks ago."

"Says you. But if the school newspaper reports that you've been caught red-handed, people are going to start wondering. There goes your reputation, Karl."

"I didn't *get* answers from them. I *gave* answers to them."

"You enjoy being thought of as a genius, don't you? Behind that modest facade, you really thrive on it. It's all you've got, really. But maybe you don't deserve your status."

Klimchock plops into the rolling chair behind his desk and lets the insults sink in. The weird part is that, except for the false accusation, he has nailed Karl, exactly. This is extremely disturbing. When a sadistic psychopath comes out with a startling, accurate insight into your soul, what do you do with the information?

"Either way, Karl, it looks like you've come to the end of your reign. The Reign of the Brain. Soon you'll just be one more doofy adolescent."

Karl shakes his head—not in despair, but to throw off confusion. This is not the time to mistake the enemy for a psychoanalyst. He can deal with his new self-knowledge later; right now, he's got a duel to fight.

In Greek mythology, Athena equips Perseus with the magical weapons he'll need to survive his encounter with Medusa. Karl has no heavenly helper, but he *does* have some useful, strategic knowledge, gained from watching hundreds of episodes of *Law and Order*. He can see what Klimchock is trying to do—apply pressure to his weak point, his pride, until he snaps and blurts out something self-incriminating, like, *I AM a genius! They MADE me help them. The small-brained idiots—they USED me. THEY'RE the criminals, not me!*

Knowing this, he disengages his emotions.

Klimchock keeps studying him, waiting for him to crack. It's embarrassing to be watched so closely. Karl looks down at his hands, wishing he could blink and rematerialize on another continent.

Maybe he should tell Samantha. If he explains what Klimchock wants him to do—if she prints it in the school newspaper—that would wreck Klimchock's plan, it would disgrace him.

And it would create a different sort of permanent record. A public proclamation of Karl's cheating, in print.

"I wonder if you've realized yet," Klimchock says loudly, jarringly, "that, even if I choose to ignore this incident, no highly selective college will admit you."

He waits for Karl to ask the obvious question, and Karl obliges him.

"Why not?"

"Because you haven't done anything for three years except get perfect grades. That won't fly, Karl."

"I've been working on independent projects outside of school."

"I don't care if you've cured cancer, AIDS, and hemor-rhoids, they still want to see that you're capable of functioning in a group. You know: plays well with others. When you have your pick of the best and the brightest, there's no reason to accept a social misfit."

This sounds true. The news would have paralyzed Karl with despair under other circumstances, but right now, it's just . . . incidental. Gravy. The icing on the cake.

"I could make that problem go away for you," Klimchock says. He rolls a yellow pencil playfully across his desk blotter with a flick of a fingernail, then rolls it back the opposite way with the other hand.

"How?"

"I can put you on the fencing team, which I coach myself. And I can write a letter of recommendation, praising your inspirational team leadership, your awesome powers of concentration, and the astonishing grace of your lunges."

The offer doesn't feel real. Klimchock's just spouting words, babbling. He would never do what he says.

"Do I sense distrust? I really can do this, Karl. And will. In exchange for you know what. You can walk out of here right now and tell your friends I just wanted to chat about colleges. There's no reason for anyone to know about any of this. You help me, and I'll help you."

"But—wouldn't that be cheating?"

Klimchock rubs his watery eyes with his pinkies, frowning. Karl can't tell if the assistant principal will see the error of his ways, or throw a stapler at him.

"I'm willing to bend the rules," Klimchock says, "just this once. In pursuit of a higher goal."

He swivels in his chair, 180 degrees, giving Karl privacy so he can decide.

Karl weighs the alternatives one more time: turn the Confederates in, or sacrifice himself for their sake. He remembers that they blackmailed him and don't deserve his loyalty. He remembers that he doesn't want to be a slimy snitch.

"I'm late for the superintendent," Klimchock says to the wall behind his desk. "I need your decision now."

Karl says, "Okay."

Klimchock swivels fast and stops himself by slapping the blotter with two flat hands.

"My decision is . . . I have to think about it."

The pink fingers on the blotter retract slowly, and turn into fists.

Mrs. D'Souza offers Karl a cookie on his way out. He doesn't hear her.

(She understands: it happens all the time.)

RULE #11: You play chess, right? Say your opponent gets you in a fork, and you're going to lose either your queen or your castle. Don't give up! Put him in check instead! Then, on his next move, he has to protect his king, not loot and pillage you. Maybe it's just delaying the inevitable--or maybe it'll save your behind! The same holds true if you get caught cheating. Sure, it looks hopeless . . . but your opponent may be vulnerable. I'll leave it at that, wink wink.

Chapter 11

hell-shocked, pale, basically blasted to pieces, Karl takes his backpack from his locker and heads out of the school. The bell sounds just as he reaches the front steps. It's the first of the lunch periods, and swarms of students follow him out.

"Karl!"

He keeps his back to her and speeds up, but the clatter of little wheels on concrete gets louder and louder, closer and closer. It's like waiting for a torpedo to hit.

"What did he say to you? What was that about?"

Samantha and her small rolling suitcase accompany him as he turns toward the corner. His main objective is not to fall apart in front of her.

"Nothing. He just wanted to talk to me about colleges."

"I seriously doubt that. You're hiding something, aren't

you? Let's see if I can guess. He wants to catch cheaters. What would he want with you? Hmmm."

Time oozes forward. Another ordeal to get through.

"Did he ask you the same thing I did? About people approaching you for help? And he swore you to secrecy?"

"Er—I shouldn't say."

"Listen, Karl, if you tell him anything, you can leak it to me, too. You *have* to."

"I'll think about it."

"Do you want to come over to my house for lunch?" she asks, out of the bluest blue. "I live right over there." She points to a pink and purple house with a great deal of decorative molding. "I could show you my room," and she winks at him, which is the second most terrifying event of the day.

"My parents are expecting me at home," he lies.

"You could call them. If you came with me, we'd have the whole house to ourselves."

"I better not," he mumbles.

She shakes her head. "I wish you didn't have to play so mysterious with me. We'll never get anywhere that way."

"Sorry."

"It's like you're always hiding something."

"I'm not."

"Yes you are." She pokes the side of his head with her index finger. "I know you're in there, secrets. Come out with your hands up."

They've come to her house. Lining the edges of the front walk like soldiers are two parallel rows of bushes, each a perfectly pruned sphere. Up on the second floor, one of the windows reveals a baby blue ceiling through sheer lavender curtains. A row of stuffed animals sits on the sill.

Her finger tickles his scalp. "You will come to my room," she says, hypnotist-style. "You will obey."

A silver Mercedes goes by, with Phillip Upchurch at the wheel. Upchurch watches them with a malevolent sort of fascination. He heard the announcement on the P.A., no doubt. Karl gets the message: *you couldn't stay out of trouble, could you? Well, I can't save you this time, moron.*

He veers away from Samantha. "Sorry. I'll see you later."

There's an ominous quiet behind him: the little wheels aren't clattering. He doesn't look back.

Just before dinner, he finds three new messages in his email, not counting the pharmaceutical spam. He opens Lizette's first.

I HOPE THE KLIMCHOCK THING WASN'T WHAT IT SOUNDED LIKE. BTW, HAPPY BIRTHDAY, LATE. I'M STILL NOT TALKING TO YOU.

If he could climb into the monitor, he would search until he found her, so he could tell her—what?

To his relief, Blaine's message doesn't contain a threat against his property or his loved ones: it's just a question mark. He deletes it without replying.

Since he can't have Lizette's sympathy, he sends Cara a note. KLIMCHOCK CAUGHT ME, TOO. THERE GOES MY LIFE.

Will she respond? *Don't hold your breath*, he advises himself.

Jonah's note, last of the three, includes a mysterious link to YouTube. When he plays the video, it's the Fabulous

Flying Stringbinis, that night on State Street. Their faces freeze in absurd, clowning expressions each time the stream buffers. He consumes the small blurred images hungrily, and when the clip ends, he plays it again.

The Quick Pick-Me-Up of Death: Jonah and Matt go flying. *"Hey!"*

"One of my high school friends went to Princeton," Karl's dad is saying, "and he used to tell crazy stories about the fraternity pranks there. Supposedly, this one guy hung naked from the top of my friend's door, and when he came back to his room, the guy grabbed his head in a naked scissor-lock. I always wondered if my friend was exaggerating."

Karl stares queasily at the highway directions on his dad's old iMac, while the printer spits out the route.

"Don't let it scare you, Karl, that was a long time ago. And he ended up liking the school a lot."

The hard wooden back of his father's spare office chair presses uncomfortably against Karl's vertebrae.

"Am I making everything worse? Sorry. Maybe I should shut my big trap."

He types in his next route request: from Princeton to the University of Pennsylvania.

"One last thing: did you know that Albert Einstein taught at Princeton? Can you wrap your brain around that?"

"Dad," Karl blurts out, "a friend of mine is in trouble. I'm worried about him."

His father goes solemn. He asks quietly, "What sort of trouble?"

"He got caught cheating on a test."

"Whew!"

His dad's cackle offends him.

"Why are you laughing?"

"Sorry—not to minimize your friend's problem—it's just that, when a son says, 'My friend is in trouble,' a parent always assumes he's talking about himself, in code. You had me scared for a minute. Go on, tell me what's up with your friend."

His father divides his attention between Karl's story and the route to Philadelphia. Karl wishes he could get his dad to listen more carefully, but he's afraid to demand it, because then his father might guess the truth.

After many *Hm*s, his father takes his fingernail from the monitor glass and says, "Your friend really got himself into a jam. I hope, if nothing else, you can learn from his mistake. Although I can't imagine you ever screwing up to that degree. Hey, look at this, it's under an hour from Princeton to Philly. We'll just have to be careful to avoid rush hour."

"What should my friend *do*, Dad? Can you give me some legal advice, that I can tell him?"

"Sorry, I don't have a clue—this is way out of my field. If he were my kid, I'd be tearing my hair out right now—and you know how I prize what's left of my hair."

While Karl mentally drills a hole toward the earth's core, in which he can hide for the rest of his life, the phone rings.

"Petrofsky and Son," his father answers. Then, "It's for you."

"I tried your cell but it's turned off," Blaine says. "And you didn't answer my email. You really shouldn't cut the lines of communication in a crisis, Carlos. So—what did Klimchock say?"

"Um, I'm here with my dad doing MapQuests."

"Understood. I'll ask yes or no questions. Did he ask for names?"

"Yes."

"Did you give him any?"

"No. I'd better go, I'll talk to you later."

"Karl, we have to know what's going on. You honestly didn't tell him anything?"

"Right. Bye."

His dad is scrutinizing the little map underneath the directions. "You can talk to your friends, I don't mind. You sounded a bit rude there, FYI."

"He's not really my friend."

"Oh."

His father zooms in on Philadelphia. While the iMac's colorful little Wheel of Waiting spins, Karl seeks refuge from the catastrophe that's hurtling toward him. The bookshelves are full of histories and biographies—no sanctuary there. Fist-size busts of Jefferson, Lincoln, and FDR stand up from the desk like strange bronze vegetation. There's also a mobile of photos showing him, Karl, at various stages of growth, all happy.

The panic swells until it bursts. "Can an assistant principal even *do* the things he's doing? Can he put signal detectors around the building? Isn't there a law against spying on people? And what about kicking people out of school and putting notes on their records? He's ruining their lives forever—how can he be allowed to do that? And making someone cheat on the SAT *can't* be legal."

Hopeful for the first time since he heard his name over the P.A., Karl clutches the spiral cord of his father's phone and eagerly awaits the verdict.

His father leans back in his chair and swivels toward Karl. "You're a good friend, to care this much. Okay, let's take your points one at a time. First—I believe the school does have the right to install surveillance devices in classrooms, because they're considered public places. And it's my understanding that the principal or assistant principal can take any disciplinary action that's appropriate, whether it's expulsion or putting a note on a transcript."

The Eagle of Hope, shot dead, lands head down in the water with a splash.

"On the other hand, he absolutely can't tell a student to cheat on the SAT. Basically, he can't do anything illegal."

What's this? A white-feathered head rising from the placid surface?

"Would that include offering to lie on a college application?" Karl asks.

"Mmm—I don't think that rises to the level of breaking the law. But it's so improper, he could be fired for it."

The brass section blares a patriotic fanfare. Our national symbol soars again!

"The problem is *proving* he said these things to your friend. Also, if your friend really did cheat, then he's in deep doo-doo no matter what happens to the assistant principal. Going public won't get him out of trouble."

Karl releases the phone cord and stares at the blotches imprinted on his palm. They look like Morse code—but if there's a message, he can't read it.

On his father's monitor, meanwhile, the route from Princeton to Philadelphia is a lavender worm with a magenta digestive tract: a squiggle connecting two places that have nothing to do with his future.

"You know, Karl," his father says, "it really doesn't matter to me which college you end up at."

"Really?"

"Seriously. *Any* of them will make me ecstatic. Princeton, Yale, Columbia—not only will they open doors for you—when people ask where my son's going to school, I'll get to say, 'Harvard,' or whatever. That's going to be one of the high points of my life."

Chapter 12

Princeton: old stone buildings, tall trees, stone archways, third largest college chapel in the world, Nassau Hall, Woodrow Wilson was president of the university before he was president of the United States, Einstein didn't actually belong to the faculty, he was at the Institute for Advanced Study, but his office was on campus, and you may recognize this courtyard from the movie *A Beautiful Mind*—John Forbes Nash Jr. still teaches here, by the way—and here's McCosh Hall, where students take their exams according to the Student Honor Code. But where *are* the students? They're sanely staying out of this pouring rain that refuses to let up, while the cheerful sophomore tour guide (native of Hong Kong) never lets the sogginess dampen her smiley spirits. She hopes to work for the U.N. someday, she says, and meanwhile plays bluegrass fiddle as a hobby.

The University of Pennsylvania: more old stone buildings, and here's the Green, you'll pass through here many times a day, there's Ben Franklin, who founded the university, and kids love to climb on the big Button (Claes Oldenberg, 1981), and did you know that ENIAC, the world's first all-electronic digital computer, was created here in the Towne Building in the 1940s, and you'd be seeing lots of Frisbees and footballs flying here on the Quad if the weather were nicer—but it's not, the April showers are threatening to drown all potential May flowers, drenching Karl and his parents, and all the stone buildings are swirling together in one big wet whirlpool, while the future that should have awaited him washes away like a sandcastle at high tide. All he wants is to close his eyes and go to sleep, he's so tired and this whole trip is so pointless—though his parents don't know it, they're beaming, damp-faced, at every historic hall and courtyard—and he hasn't slept well in days, but he drifts off in the car, and when he wakes up, they're pulling off the turnpike and he's sweating and coughing, and when he wakes up the next morning he has a high fever and chills, he can barely catch his breath, he keeps coughing painfully, and when he spits out the gunk, the mucus is pale green.

The symptoms last all weekend. He's achingly tired, and on Monday an X-ray shows he's got pneumonia—and not just that, the lining of his lungs is inflamed, a condition known as pleurisy. That's why it hurts so much every time he coughs—which means he can't bring up the mucus and clear his lungs the way he needs to—which means, according to Dr. Dahesh, that his best bet is to spend a few days in the hospital for a course of antibiotics.

No longer a pediatric patient, Karl has an older roommate in the hospital, a soft-spoken, white-haired man named Mr. Hydine, who has no noticeable symptoms. In the middle of the night, though, Mr. Hydine turns into Dr. Jekylline, screaming, *"Help!"* hoarsely, hysterically, repeatedly. Karl can't leap out of bed and help him, because he's got an intravenous tube in his arm he can't even see his roommate from inside his ripply gold curtain—for all he knows, the guy has turned into a werewolf—but he pushes the Nurse Call button and shouts through the curtain, "It's okay, Mr. Hydine, I called the nurse, she'll be right here."

The nurse doesn't show up right away, though, and Mr. Hydine keeps screaming, so Karl tries again, "Mr. Hydine, what's wrong? Is there anything I can do?" to which Mr. Hydine sobs, "They're trying to kill me." Though dubious, Karl asks, "Who is?" and Mr. Hydine replies, "All of you," moaning tearfully until the nurse finally arrives and calms the old man with gentle words.

"He just gets confused and agitated in the dark," she explains to Karl.

As if to prove her right, Mr. Hydine repeats his terrifying performance three more times that first night.

A painful tug on his arm wakes Karl at 7 A.M. A different nurse is administering his antibiotic through the IV line, and she has carelessly backed against the tube that leads to Karl's forearm. "Good morning, Karl," Mr. Hydine says pleasantly.

All of this explains why, when his parents come to visit, Karl looks even more haggard than he did when he entered the hospital.

He's so wiped out that he can be forgiven for sleeping through Jonah and Matt's visit, and Blaine's phone call. When Samantha calls, he tells her that Mr. Klimchock just came to see him and threatened him with a knife. "Ha ha ha," Samantha replies, which helps Karl understand that he dreamed the visit. ("Such a disappointing spring break." Samantha sighs. "All this rain, and you sick, and you not calling me once. Very sad.")

He tries to reach Cara, but the number has been disconnected.

Waking from a nap, he finds a note written on a napkin on his lunch tray.

> Your conscience is telling you something.
> Listen to it! I miss my friend —L.

Happy and excited, he picks up the phone to call her but hangs up before dialing because what can he say? If he tells her about Klimchock's coercion, she'll get so outraged that she might try to expose it in public, and then the whole thing would explode in his face.

Still, he misses her, and keeps the note in his hands, and wonders what she really thinks of him, and what he would want, if it were a possibility, even though it's not.

Cough, cough. Cough cough cough. Pain. Grimacing.

"You can ask for a painkiller, you know," says Mr. Hydine.

"I can?"

"No point suffering unnecessarily."

That sounds like wisdom, even if it comes from a midnight maniac. He presses his Nurse Call button, and almost instantly, a frowning beauty appears at his bedside. Francesca Subitsky, her ID card says. She has short blond hair, rectangular glasses, rosy cheeks, a perky nose, and a massive copy of *Bride's* magazine in her hand.

"Yes?" she asks impatiently.

"My chest—when I cough, it hurts a lot. Would it be okay if I took a Tylenol?"

"Sure," she says brusquely, and stomps away. She comes back with a pill in a paper cup, saying, "Here."

"Thanks for the advice," Karl says to Mr. Hydine when she's gone, but the old guy has fallen asleep. Karl doesn't want to wake him, so he leaves the TV off and tries reading the dusty, yellowed science fiction paperbacks his dad brought, *Dune* and *Stranger in a Strange Land.* Trouble is, the books leave huge empty regions in his brain where dark visions of his future unfold—mopping floors? welcoming drive-thru customers to Burger King?—and so he puts the books down and plays with the bed's controls, trying to see how many different angles and shapes he can make with the mattress, and when he has his feet up high, his back flat, and his butt in a deep trough, Phillip Upchurch walks into the room.

"Comfortable?" Upchurch asks. He's wearing white tennis shorts and a white polo shirt, and as Karl returns the bed to a simple obtuse angle, he surveys the remains of Karl's lunch on the rolling tray: the yellow Jell-O, the limp, oily fries, the crusts of white bread, the sad, putrid green beans in diagonally sliced segments.

"Hi," Karl mumbles. "What are you doing here? Are you a volunteer?"

"Not this year."

An odd smell reaches Karl, sort of like the air freshener his family keeps in the bathroom, a foresty scent with some lemon in it.

Upchurch's cologne.

"How are you feeling?"

"Not too bad," Karl says, and coughs, once, twice, thrice. He tries to speak, but the rest of his coughing fit prevents him, rattling his ribs, making him wince, until he's got a mouthful of gunk that must be gotten rid of, not swallowed. He spits it into the curved plastic pan the nurse left by his bedside the first day. "How are you?"

Upchurch, stiff-backed, grimaces.

Karl's head is too clogged to think of a polite way to ask the visitor why he has come, but the answer arrives soon enough. Upchurch wanders to the door, peers up and down the hall, and comes back in—an odd thing to do, but not as odd as when he waves at Mr. Hydine's face. The old man keeps snoring.

"What's going on?" Karl asks.

"I'm going crazy because no one knows how much you told Klimchock."

Karl watches the gold curtain sway languorously in Upchurch's breeze. Maybe he's in some sort of pneumonia-induced hallucinogenic stupor.

"You have to tell me, Karl. This is serious."

"Why do you want to know?"

(Because he might be a spy: not a secret member of the

Confederacy, but an informer sent by Klimchock to imper-sonate a cheater.)

Upchurch spreads out the three hip-hop CDs Karl's mother brought—a salesman's recommendation, the polar oppo-site of Karl's musical taste. Shaking his head disdainfully, he explains: "I told Blaine to recruit you because I didn't trust any of those morons to come up with the right answers. Before you joined the group, Blaine screwed up on a chemis-try test—he spelled *Avogadro* wrong, so the rest of us did, too. Luckily Nudell was out sick that week and Grantley marked her papers for her. Do you have any idea what would have happened if Nudell caught us all writing *Abogado*? We would have fried. But Grantley didn't notice—or didn't care."

Upchurch has pimples that Karl never noticed before, because they're covered by a cream that matches his flesh perfectly. His eyebrows are thick and lie along a prominent ridge; they don't meet in the middle, but Karl suspects a tweezer may have been involved.

The surface of Upchurch is all he can bear to explore. What lies beneath is too awful to think about. (That story about wanting to beat out Karl for valedictorian—did he make that up on the spot, as a cover-up, or is it still true? Karl can't judge, he's too dizzy and confused.)

"Shocked?" Upchurch asks. "Get over it."

"I just thought you really were smart."

Letting that pass, Upchurch says, "For the record, I didn't organize this to benefit myself. It's for the whole town."

The claim is so preposterous, there's no way to challenge it without calling Upchurch a liar. "I don't see how that could possibly be true."

"Then listen: the school's standardized test scores have been going down, and that's affecting the real estate market. *New Jersey Magazine* didn't include our school in its Top Fifty last year. No one's going to pay a million for a four-bedroom house in a town where the high school sucks. Now do you understand?"

Karl is lost as a lamb in a dark labyrinth, but he can't bring himself to admit it. "Sort of."

A deep sigh, a roll of the eye. "My father's going to run for mayor in November. You know who he is, right? Randall Upchurch? Cathedral Realty?"

"Uh-huh."

Mr. Hydine groans in his sleep and says, "Please—no!" Upchurch freezes, and waits until the snoring resumes.

"Okay, I'll spell it out for you. Raise the school's SAT scores and you raise the value of every house in town."

"But, for that to happen, *lots* of people would have to be part of the Confederacy. And they're not."

"Oh, they are. Just because they keep a low profile, that doesn't mean they're all playing it straight."

"But I only saw"—he counts on his fingers—". . . six people cheat. Plus you."

"A lot goes on under the surface. The point is, the principal knows all about it, and he *wants* us to cheat, because that way he can keep his job, which he wouldn't if everyone got scores like last year's."

Karl can't decide whether or not he should believe a word Upchurch has said. On the one hand, anything's possible. On the other, if the whole school has been cheating and the principal approves, that's just too . . . hideous.

But he doesn't want Upchurch to know he's upset. "Aside from the property values, I guess the higher grades won't hurt when you apply to colleges."

"Are you insulting me? Are you saying I'm really doing it just for myself? Is that what you're saying?"

"I'm not sure. Maybe. I don't know."

"That's right, Karl. You really don't know much about anything."

A cell phone rings, playing "Hail to the Chief." Upchurch checks the caller's number and moves to the doorway. He keeps his back to Karl. "What? . . . The Friendly Kitchen doesn't *have* a security person, how can they ask volunteers for ID? . . . That's insane . . . Well—just tell them you lost your wallet, you don't have any ID on you. Look, figure it out. I'm not going to pay you if you don't sign me in, obviously."

Uninformed and ill though Karl may be, he's able to piece together these clues. A profile in *The Emancipator* last fall reported that Upchurch volunteered at the Rainbow After-school Center, tutoring little kids; at the Ida and Bob Jergenson Senior Center, visiting with the elderly; and at the Friendly Kitchen, serving hot meals to the homeless. Karl wondered back then how one person could find the time to do so much, on top of his many other activities. Now he has the answer: someone else has been serving those hot meals and signing Upchurch's name. Chances are he has similar arrangements at the Afterschool and Senior centers.

Though Karl never speaks the insult aloud—*You sleazebag!*—it must be legible on his face.

"There are reasons for everything I do, Karl. And I don't go around breaking rules unless it's absolutely necessary."

"How is faking community service absolutely necessary?"

"If you want to go to an Ivy League school and you're not an athlete or the son of an alumnus, it's *totally* necessary. There aren't that many slots, Karl—and the applicants are all superhuman. They don't just win every competition they enter—they deliver medicine to sick Eskimos by dogsled, and play the oboe with the New York Philharmonic. You would know all this if you ever lifted your head out of whatever stupid comic book you waste your time on."

The more Upchurch talks, the more Karl wishes he had the physical strength to punch him in the nose. Since he doesn't, and since Upchurch's cologne is starting to make him sick to his stomach, he asks bluntly, "Why did you come here?"

Again, Upchurch waves at Mr. Hydine's unconscious face and peeks up and down the hall. He leans in close to Karl so no one else will hear.

"I have to know what you told Klimchock. And I need you to help us with the SAT."

If Upchurch thinks Karl will help him after all his insults, then Upchurch's brain has a serious defect. Karl laughs at him contemptuously—but this proves to be a painful mistake, because it triggers another coughing fit.

"What if I don't help you?" he chokes out.

"You'll be squashed like a worm under a boot. Bad things will happen to you. But that's not how it's going to be. You're going to help us."

Why does his tone of voice sound so familiar? Wait— could it be? Yes—he's modeling himself, confusingly, on

Klimchock. It's as if the Joker's son became Batman's new sidekick.

"Take a look at this," Upchurch says. From the pocket of his shorts, he removes . . . a number two pencil.

Karl withholds his admiration.

"Don't judge a pencil by its looks. This is not your father's Dixon Ticonderoga. Look here."

His fingernail points to a small opening in the ferrule, the metal part that holds the eraser on.

"Take a feel."

He hands Karl the pencil. It's heavy—as if it were made of steel, not wood.

"That opening is a lens. Inside this pencil—which you can also use to write your answers—is a compact, state-of-the-art cheating machine. First, it recognizes letters and numbers. Second, it generates a voice that speaks the number of the question and the letter you darkened. Third, it transmits the message to whoever's listening by earphone. You fill in the answers, then sweep the lens over them, and the Magic Pencil does the rest. The only thing missing is a human brain to supply the right answers."

So far, Karl has taken all of Upchurch's bullying like . . . like . . . a sick person in a hospital. The time has come to fight back.

"What if I say no—and if you do anything to me, then I'll turn you in as the biggest cheater of all, and a community service fraud?"

An effortless parry: "Sorry, but there's no evidence against me, and you're already in disgrace. Anything you say will sound like desperate raving."

Outside, the rain has left shadowy stains on the concrete wall across the airshaft. The uneaten part of Karl's lunch is growing more repulsive by the minute.

"I don't have all day, Karl. What did you tell Klimchock?"

He can't see a way out. No matter what he does, it will end in disaster.

He sucks his lips in, thinking, thinking.

"Don't smirk at me. Did you give him any names or not?"

Karl doesn't know what to say and doesn't want to give any information away just in case.

Upchurch eyes Karl's IV tube. He wouldn't yank it—would he?

"You're *not* going to mess me up."

He takes one of the three CDs Karl's mother brought and waves it in Karl's face. "You want me to get your old pals thrown out of school? Is that what you want?"

Karl yawns—not for theatrical effect but because he's intensely tired.

In a fit, out of control, Upchurch snatches all three CDs from the rolling tray and pitches them into the round hole of the red biohazard bin.

The message seems to be, *I'll do the same to you if you don't obey me.*

Nurse Francesca is standing in the doorway. "I saw that. You can't play adolescent pranks in here—your friend is sick. What's wrong with you?"

"Shut up!" Upchurch screams.

"*Shut up?* Okay, Mister, you're out of here. Say good-bye. And you owe him three CDs—I'm a witness."

Upchurch says, "You—" but holds back the rest. He tells

Karl, "Next time I come, you'd better give me the answer I want to hear."

Nurse Francesca takes out her cell phone and snaps a picture of Upchurch. "There won't be a next time: you're not coming back. I don't like the way you talk to my patients. This picture is going to the security desk downstairs. Sayonara, creep."

Upchurch lets out a growl that consists entirely of the letter r: "Rrrrrrrrrrrr!"

By the time the growl ends, he's gone.

"Are you really friends with that jerk?" the nurse asks Karl.

"No—the opposite. Thanks for throwing him out."

"Oh, I enjoyed it."

Mr. Hydine yawns, opens his eyes, and smiles at Karl and Nurse Francesca. "The sun finally came out, I see."

At first, Karl thinks the old man is hallucinating again, but a glance out the window shows that Mr. Hydine is right. The sky above the gray concrete has turned pale blue again, the clouds are bright white.

"Hallelujah," says Nurse Francesca.

Karl wishes he, too, could find cheer in the sunny sky. For him, though, the gray gloom is permanent and inescapable.

RULE #13: Learn from the martial arts: turn the force of your enemy's attack into the force that defeats him. The hard part is figuring out how to do this when you're caught and threatened with suspension. Personally, it didn't work for me--I got thrown out of my last school for trying--but it's still a cool concept. Maybe you can make it work.

Chapter 13

After Mr. Hydine's discharge from the hospital, Karl misses the old guy's company—for about three minutes. Then he falls asleep.

He dreams he's wandering down a rocky hillside, into a meadow filled with tall dry grass—a pleasant place, until soldiers start shooting at him, first from the edge of the woods, then from behind the rocks on the opposite side. He understands that they're not really after him, they're fighting each other (ragged gray uniforms versus ragged blue uniforms), but these are not noble soldiers, they're tough, dirty, and sadistic, and they couldn't care less if he gets shot. So he's running every which way, searching for a hole he can dive into, but every time he spots one, it turns out to be just a shadow. "I'm not *in* this!" he shouts at them, pleading for mercy.

His own shout wakes him up. He discovers that he has tangled his sheet in a truly artistic manner. He's curled on his side, and there's someone watching him from alongside the bed—a girl in a black sweatshirt with chestnut hair in a short bowl. This confuses him, because Lizette's hair looked different, shorter, the last time he saw it. Also, she almost always kept it covered with a baseball cap.

"See what happens when you do bad things?" she says. "Eternal torment."

Almost giddy with happiness, he's about to say, *You broke your vow—you talked to me*—but he notices that his hands are on top of his head. Why is that? Because he was dodging bullets a moment ago.

Unscrunching himself, he fixes the sheet so he's covered up to the neck. "Hi," he says.

His joy at the sight of her is complicated by shame— because the friend who begged him not to do wrong has returned to find him demolished by his mistake, and she has also seen his underwear, exposed by the twisted hospital gown. He peers at her face, and down at his hands, and back at her face, and down at his hands, and so on.

Lizette has her own confusions and can't look him in the eye. She picks up the framed snapshot of him with his parents (squinting at the beach) and says, "This is the best picture they could find of y'all?"

"We're not that photogenic."

He wishes he could kiss her and hug her, but instead they make small talk.

"So how did your spring break go?" she asks. "Catch up on your rest?"

"Uh-huh. How about you?"

"Pretty dull. A little day trip with the family to Cooperstown, the Hall of Fame, that was nice. You see the error of your ways yet?"

Heart full to bursting, he holds his troubles inside.

He can't remember, though, why he's keeping it all to himself. Therefore, he blurts out everything—the whole nasty tale of Klimchock's coercion and Upchurch's secret life as the Prince of Sleaze.

He assumes she'll sympathize, but her face goes cold and distant as he speaks. Maybe she's saving her compassion for the end.

Or, maybe not.

"I can't believe you ever got involved with them, Karl. You should have known better. The whole thing is so low-down."

"I told you, I wish I never started."

The A/C cycles on, and goose bumps form on Karl's forearms.

"You dug your own grave, Karl. It's nobody's fault but yours."

By refusing to give him the slightest bit of sympathy, Lizette leaves Karl deeply disappointed. Also, to tell the truth, annoyed.

"Klimchock called Jonah into his office today," she says.

"Why?"

"He said Jonah was cheating."

"*What?!*"

"You know Jonah's nervous tic, where he turns his neck to the side? Klimchock said he was copying from his neighbor's test."

Thinking, thinking . . . Is it a ploy, a message to Karl? *Give in or I'll crush everyone you care about.* Or maybe that's delusional.

"What happened? Did he get expelled?"

"He got sent home with all his stuff. I helped him empty his locker."

"How upset was he?"

"How upset do you think?"

That Klimchock would blackmail Karl is one thing. At least Karl really cheated. But Jonah . . .

"So what are you planning to do?" she asks.

"I don't have a clue. I wish I could run away and join the circus."

"There aren't too many job openings for a lone Flying Stringbini."

Lunch arrives. Karl and Lizette stare at the pale bread and the green curls of lettuce sticking out past the crust, all strangled by tight plastic wrap.

"They're just evil," Lizette says. "Both of them—Klimchock and Upchurch. They deserve to sink in their own vile sludge."

These are the first kind words she has spoken to Karl in a long time—but they don't solve the problem, because there is no solution.

A second visitor interrupts their gloom-fest. This one has on a red tank top, tight capris, and red sunglasses worn up above her forehead, right on top of her silky dark bangs, which are new.

"Hello, everybody," Cara says.

Karl and Lizette are helpless to do anything but stare.

"I heard you were here. Just wanted to stop by and see how everything's going."

"I tried to call you, but the number was disconnected," Karl says.

"We moved to a different apartment. I'm working in my aunt's hardware store."

Lizette drifts away, over toward the sink. Cara stands at the foot of the bed. In a way, Karl's a lucky guy. Two girls he likes both cared about him enough to visit him in the hospital. They would both go out of their way to help him—but they can't get him out of this predicament, no one can, it's hopeless, and not just for him, for Jonah, too.

Tears trickle down his cheeks before he can stop them.

"Hey, Edison, what's up? Why'd you spring a leak?"

Since Karl can't make his voice work, Lizette explains matters to Cara. Through his teary blur, Karl notices something odd: Lizette never looks Cara in the face. He wonders, could Lizette have a crush on Cara? Was all her criticizing just a way of covering it up?

Cara knocks that thought out of his head with a loud laugh. *"Phillip Upchurch? He's Blaine's secret overlord? The up-sucking weasel with the pole up his butt?"*

She lets out a snort.

"That's *hilarious.* I can just see Blaine—'Yes, sir, Your Oiliness.' That's the funniest thing I've heard all year."

Karl isn't laughing, though. His attention has returned to the matter at hand—how Klimchock's cruelty and injustice are matched only by Upchurch's fraudulence and general disgustingness. They both deserve to be exposed.

The seed of an idea sprouts instantly: he'll do it. He'll tell the world the truth about both of them, no matter the consequences. It needs to be done.

"There's no way out of this," he says. "My future is already wrecked. I'm going to expose them both."

"Hold on," says Cara. "There's one little problem: nobody will believe you. We'd better stop and think this over."

The three of them ponder Karl's plight in silence.

"This is so frustrating," Lizette comments.

They're stumped. Nurse Francesca finds them moping together when she comes to administer Karl's afternoon antibiotics. She teases Karl while setting the dosage on the IV computer. "Uh-oh, looks like they found out about each other. It's dangerous, being a ladies' man."

Lizette turns a sunburned red. Not Cara, though. "I don't mind sharing him," she says. "As long as I get him half the time."

"If I weren't engaged," Francesca says, "I might want to find out what all the excitement's about."

Karl blushes redder than Lizette and scrutinizes his own lap. He doesn't see that Lizette's face has puckered into a tormented little cluster of features. Cara, on the other hand, not only sees, but understands.

Discreetly, she backs away from the bed and joins Lizette at the sink. Lizette moves away from her—as Cara knew she would—and ends up back at the bed.

As soon as Francesca leaves, Cara says, "If you really want to expose them, you'll need proof."

"That sure is helpful," Lizette complains. "What should he do, go back in time with a tape recorder?"

"You're going to have to wear a wire, Karl, and get them to repeat what they said."

Lizette ridicules the idea. "This isn't TV. Real people don't wear wires. And even if Karl somehow got them to speak right into the microphone, I still don't like the idea of him messing up his whole life."

"That's because you care about him so much," Cara answers, smiling.

Jerked alert, suspended in the still space between two heartbeats, Karl focuses eyes and soul on Lizette.

She pretends that Cara didn't say anything unusual or life-altering. "No, really—I just wish—I wish there were a way for Karl to *duck* and let them fire away at each other."

It's intriguing to Karl how closely this thought resembles his dream, the one with the blue and gray soldiers firing across the meadow, and him in the middle. To him, this means that their minds are connected—complementary.

Wanting to earn her respect, he works out his plan in detail: he will do as Cara says, get the proof, and then mail it to newspapers and local TV stations. Maybe he'll give Samantha a copy, too. He always wanted to undermine the unjust powers that be; now he can do it for real. If, that is, he can get them on tape.

He admits his uncertainty to his friends. "I just don't know if a regular person can do this sort of thing."

Cara reassures him. "You're not a regular person, Karl. Never were and never will be."

Lizette adds an encouragement of her own. "I guess it's like my daddy says: you can't climb out of a hole without getting dirty."

She forces herself to look him in the eye, and she's rewarded for her courage, because, with two girls to choose from, he's gazing into *her* eyes, not Cara's.

Certain confusing questions are beginning to get answered here. Just as some chemical reactions produce heat, this rapid sorting-out produces powerful emotions—powerful enough to send Lizette's hand over to where Karl's foot is poking up under the sheet. What, he wonders, will it do there?

She holds his big toe through the sheet. His ecstasy is so complete that he doesn't notice Cara leaving, even though she's humming a song—a very familiar song, which Karl and Lizette hear as background music.

Can you guess? Can you deduce? Can you feel the love tonight?

RULE #14: Most people, when they're caught, decide it's too dangerous to ever cheat again. (Cowards!) But if you're one of the few, the brave, the pure of (cheating) heart, you have my respect. Just keep your eyes open, including the ones in the back of your head, because they'll be watching you like an amoeba under a microscope.

Chapter 14

Karl's parents are kissing him good-bye the next day when Lizette returns to the hospital room. She's wearing a plain white T-shirt and cutoff jeans with the fringes just above her knees. Her legs and arms, which Karl has never seen before, are long, lean, and full of goose bumps. *She's beautiful*, he thinks.

A short, stocky man follows her in, wearing a bright blue T-shirt, baggy red shorts, and white socks up to his knees. This can't possibly be her father (first, how could this little guy have produced such a tall daughter, not to mention her two titanic brothers? and second, he looks ridiculous!) but that's exactly who he is. Lizette introduces him to Karl and his parents, and the first words out of Mr. Frenais's mouth, directed at Mr. and Mrs. Petrofsky as he shakes their hands, are, "Sorry to hear about all this trouble of yours."

Funny, isn't it, how a lightning bolt can strike from a cloudless sky, when you're worried about a completely different catastrophe, and leave you charred, with a jagged mouth and only one crooked wisp of hair remaining?

"What do you mean?" Karl's father asks.

Karl had been recovering nicely from his illness, but now he breaks into a drenching sweat.

Honest, sincere Lizette invents the quickest cover-up Karl has ever seen. "Daddy, you're confusing Karl with my other friend, the one who got hit by that ice-cream truck. Karl's fine, he's just getting over pneumonia. Please don't scare his parents."

"Oh. Ohhhhh. Sorry about that. Well—glad to meet you."

"You had me scared for a minute." Karl's father laughs. "Whew!"

Exit the chuckling parents. On with the intrigue.

Mr. Frenais knows all about Karl's situation. He has come with Lizette to help set up the hidden microphone, the one she bought online yesterday, paying an extra fifteen dollars for overnight delivery. (The mike is a tiny black box with a switch, not much bigger than the nine-volt battery that fits inside it.) Though Mr. Frenais agreed to help, Karl keeps expecting him to deliver a lecture about honesty; the lecture never comes, however.

The mike works best when the mesh screen points directly at the speaker's mouth. Mounting it on Karl's nose would be ideal, but since that might not be the best location, secrecy-wise, they experiment with other options.

Placing the mike inside Karl's hospital gown doesn't work. "All I could hear was fabric rubbing on it," Mr. Frenais says. "And stomach-gurgling." He suggests gluing the mike to Karl's scalp and concealing it inside Karl's floppy mop of hair. Sounds a bit silly, but they give it a go. After fluffing Karl's hair to hide the mike, Mr. Frenais goes out in the hall and listens on his earphone as Lizette says, "So, Karl, I hope you've learned your lesson."

He's still fumbling for an answer when Mr. Frenais comes back into the room with two thumbs up, announcing, "Loud and clear."

A difficult question remains, though: how to attach the mike to Karl's scalp? "We've got a hot glue gun at home," Lizette offers.

"I'm thinking this looks like a job for rubber cement," says Mr. Frenais, and off he goes to the nearest Staples, one town over, leaving his daughter and Karl to . . . um . . . er. . . .

The last time we saw them together, Cara had bluntly announced that Lizette *cared about Karl so much.* Lizette's electrifying grip on his toe lasted a long time; neither of them could think of what to say next, and Lizette never moved her hand. If the loud guy in blue scrubs hadn't appeared to collect the garbage, they might still be there, toe in fist; but as soon as he popped his head in and blared, "How's everybody today?" Lizette dashed out the door.

And now they're together again, just the two of them,

and he knows he has to say something, *do* something, make his feelings known, or else she'll think he wants to be *just friends*.

He summons his courage. He speaks.

"Um, I'll pay you back for the mike."

"You definitely will."

"Thanks for getting it. And for bringing your father."

"No problem. Glad to help."

He's run out of words. She pops a piece of Orbit gum into her mouth and turns her back to him. He's not sure what that means, but it can't be good.

Except that it helps: not having to look her in the eye makes it possible to speak again. "I've been wanting to say to you—ever since the first day when you showed up at school—I like you so much. But I kind of thought—I think a lot of people thought—that you . . ."

She keeps her back turned but cocks her ear to make sure she hears the end of the sentence.

". . . were gay," he mumbles, fearfully.

She whirls around. Her face has turned Red Lobster red.

"*What?!* Why? Because I like sports? Because I don't wear quarts of makeup, or dress like Cara?"

"No, none of that. I don't know . . ."

She stalks over to the door. "I don't *want* to act like that, or dress like that. It's never gonna happen. What's that got to do with anything, anyway? Does a person *have* to be like her to be accepted? And y*ou*—how could—"

She's too upset to limit herself to one thought at a time—too upset to speak. It looks to Karl as if she might just run away. Panicking—not because he needs her help with the hidden mike, but because she *can't* leave this way, before she even knows how he feels—he blurts out, "I kept wishing you *weren't* gay. I'm not even sure anymore why I thought it. I was stupid."

"That's an understatement."

An old man in a wheelchair goes past the doorway, peeking in. When he's out of sight, Lizette kicks the doorframe with her sneaker and says a quiet, "Ow."

"Are you okay?"

"Yeah. I think."

She's far away from him, and still angry. Maybe she's too angry to ever forgive him; otherwise, wouldn't she come back to him?

The disappointment silences him, until he remembers what Cara said: *That's because you care about him so much.*

Powered by the last grain of hope left inside him, he asks, "Was Cara right? About you liking me?"

"Yeah. Uh-huh." She's focusing on the little opening in the doorframe where the latch fits in. "I like being around you. I never know what's going to come out of your mouth— some comment that I have to think about and figure out a half hour later. When you're not saying something that sends me into a raging fit, that is."

"That's the best thing anybody ever said to me."

Lizette smiles, a long line with a little hook at the end, but she still avoids looking at him.

It would be reasonable to assume that they'll finally let go of their doubts and insecurities and lunge at each other now. But it's not that simple, not for these two. When you're really shy—really, *really* shy—even this much reassurance isn't quite enough.*

"Tell you what," Lizette says. "Can we just pretend we didn't say any of this stuff, till after the test?"

"Okay, but why?"

"Because we need our heads on straight for the next few days."

Karl agrees. *She's so wise and mature,* he thinks.

While they wait for Mr. Frenais to come back with the rubber cement, Lizette wanders back to the hospital bed. Discreetly, she walks two fingers onto the sheet until they reach his hand. There, on his palm, the two fingers do a little Rockettes-style dance. Neither of them knows what to do next—so they're both relieved when Mr. Frenais walks in with the Staples bag and says, "That was easy."

A good dad, he pretends he sees nothing as Lizette rockets backward, away from Karl. Then it's back to business:

---

*Noted psychologist Waldo S. Tutwiler comments: "Among those who fall in love and idolize the loved one, but don't have a high opinion of themselves, there is a strong and logical belief that the beloved moves on an elevated plane, far higher than the lowly land where they themselves dwell—so how could the adored one possibly return their feelings? The advice I give to my young clients in such cases is that this whole way of thinking is a self-destructive mistake. Yes, I tell them, go ahead and desire the appealing person—but stop thinking you're a toad by comparison! There's no need to grovel in the mud. Besides, from a purely practical point of view, this attitude will destroy any chance you may have of forming a real relationship. Stand at your full height and meet the loved one's gaze with dignity. Then, and only then, will you have a chance at romantic happiness." [Author's Note: Learn from Dr. Tutwiler and you may be able to save yourself years of heartache and thousands of dollars in therapy bills. If only Karl could read this!]

brushing the viscous rubber cement onto the bottom of the microphone, parting Karl's hair to clear a narrow runway of scalp, pressing the mike firmly into place, and artfully arranging Karl's hair around it. While pressing down on the mike and waiting for the cement to dry, Mr. Frenais says, "I'm curious about one thing, Karl."

"What's that?"

"I'm wondering, can you tell me, in fifty words or less, why you don't want to go through life cheating?"

Mr. Frenais has short gray hair that stands straight up. He looks like a retired astronaut, or a little general, and has a rough, hoarse voice—you can easily imagine him yelling orders at his football team—but he asks this question in a kindly way, almost like a minister. That's good, because Karl knows this is a test, which will either win him Mr. Frenais's support or provoke his eternal disapproval. As calmly as he can, he thinks and speaks.

"I guess, more than anything else, it's about what kind of person you want to be," he says.

"You're sure that's the reason?"

With sinking hopes, Karl replies, "I think so, uh-huh."

"Pretty good answer," Mr. Frenais says, and takes a break from holding the mike in place so he can shake Karl's hand. "I was thinking more along the lines of, if you cheat, you have to always worry about someone catching you, and that's not the best way to live—but I like what you said, too."

Mr. Frenais's hand is rough and calloused, but Karl is so relieved, he'd gladly keep shaking it all day.

Mr. Frenais, however, goes back to pressing on the mike, and adds a P.S.: "'Course, all this sneakin' around wouldn't be necessary if you'd done the right thing in the first place. But nobody's perfect. Except my little girl here."

After a long fifteen minutes, Karl can nod and even shake his head without dislodging the microphone. Both Lizette and her father swear they can't see a trace of it through his hair. The two Frenaises say good-bye for now; Lizette waggles two fingers, reminding him of her little dance on his hand.

As soon as he's alone, Karl's innards swish like dirty laundry around an agitator. What if he can't get Klimchock and Upchurch to say what he needs them to say? What if he tries too hard and they get suspicious, or if he sweats so much that his hair gets soaked and flat, exposing the microphone? If they see it, they'll reach in and tear Karl's liver out. An infinite number of things could go wrong—but worse than any *What if* is the one thing that's certain. No college will accept a convicted cheater.

Maybe he'd better start paying attention to those commercials for technical schools, the ones where, each time you learn how to use a tool, it goes in your toolbox.

Lizette calls Mr. Klimchock at the school and Phillip Upchurch at his house, and delivers the message that Karl is still in the hospital, and he thinks he's too sick to take the test.

They wait together for the first visitor to show up. Each time they hear the elevator bell go *dong*, they look at each other with a grim sort of gaze, *This is it, the moment of truth.* Frankly, it gets pretty absurd after a while. A dozen strangers wander past the doorway—a dozen grim gazes—but then, just as Karl lets out a little snort at the comedy of it all, their first visitor shows up.

It's an Upchurch, but not Phillip.

Randall Upchurch, Realtor and candidate for mayor, could pass for a male model, thirty years later (except, perhaps, for the shape of his head, which reminds Karl of a paramecium). His creamy white suit shows off the depth of his tan—which, to tell the truth, has sort of an orange tint, unless that's a reflection from his peach-colored shirt. He wears his thinning hair combed straight back, and his teeth are as white as a new ream of paper.

"Karl Petrofsky?" he asks.

Karl nods.

"Randy Upchurch, glad to meet you."

He shakes Karl's hand firmly but cordially. Lizette is about to slip out of the room when the other elevator *dongs*, and they hear a familiar urgent rhythm: Mr. Klimchock's heavy-footed approach.

Karl and Lizette exchange a panicked glance *(Both at once?!)* and then Klimchock is there in the doorway in his standard gray suit, frowning impatiently.

Karl's stomach slides a bit to the side as Mr. Upchurch's cologne surrounds him.

While Karl's soul thrashes in a helpless panic, Mr. Klimchock's frown evolves into a fit of confused consternation. His shining, smooth scalp turns deep pink. He can't speak.

"Klimmy!" Mr. Upchurch laughs. "How's the education biz? Still molding America's future, one pimple at a time?"

Mr. Klimchock's mouth opens, but no words come out. His cheek twitches.

Another *dong*—and Samantha Abrabarba enters the room, carrying a small turquoise gift bag. She's wearing lavender slacks today, and a yellow blouse with a big foofy front. It seems to Karl that she must go through lipstick and eye makeup by the vat.

"I thought I'd have you to myself, cutie-pie," she says, taking in the crowd. "Mind if I cut in front?" she asks Mr. Upchurch, and hands Karl the gift bag. Inside, a Beanie Babies stegosaurus peeks out, with plaid fur. She leans over and kisses Karl on the cheek while he sends Lizette a scrunch-browed grimace—*She's crazy, I don't even like her*—but Lizette misses the signal because she's glaring at the floor.

"You're a popular young man," Mr. Upchurch says.

No need to reply, because Samantha takes over. "This is peculiar," she says, eyeing the two older men. "What are you two doing here?"

The assistant principal and Mr. Upchurch dart evasive glances around the room.

"What does Phillip Upchurch have to do with Karl?" Samantha wonders out loud. "And why would Mr. Klim-chock come visit you in the hospital?"

Lizette moves to the foot of Karl's bed and addresses them all crankily. "Listen, y'all—Karl is still sick, in case you didn't notice. You can't come in here all together, you'll wear him out and then he'll have a relapse. Could we get some cooperation here?"

Samantha gives Lizette a suspicious sidelong gaze. "Karl, why is she bossing everybody around? Do you want to whisper anything in my ear?"

"No, everything's fine."

"I smell something fishy. Why would they all be here together?"

Mr. Upchurch lets out an extremely fake guffaw. Mr. Klimchock follows his lead with a strained *Hmp hmp hmp.*

"You're not fooling me," Samantha says dryly.

"Will you please just—*be quiet!*" blurts Lizette.

"No, and you can't make me."

"Young lady," Mr. Upchurch says benevolently, "we're just here to visit Karl. We're not sinisterly plotting anything."

She leans in close—so close that Karl can smell her mint toothpaste—and murmurs, "What's going on, Karl? Tell me so I can rescue you!"

"Nothing's going on, they're just visiting."

"Okay, people," Lizette announces, "here's what we're going to do. We're gonna take turns. Everybody will get to see Karl, one by one, okay? No mob scenes, just nice, private conversations. You'll all get your turn. Eenie-meenie-minie-mo—you first," and she points at Mr. Upchurch. "The rest of us'll wait outside—there's a bench at the end of the hall. Let's go. Come on, before visiting hours are over."

She steers Samantha out the door with a hand on her shoulder, and gives Mr. Klimchock's suit sleeve a tug as well. Karl's heart fills with admiration and gratitude.

"That's one macho young lady," Upchurch comments. "I assume she's not your girlfriend."

"Not exactly. Not yet. Maybe, sort of."

The unexpected answer amuses Upchurch, but only briefly. Taking his time, he peeks out the doorway, just as his son did. Karl waits for him to come closer before coaxing the words from him—but Mr. Upchurch never gets near him.

"I supposed Klimmy's here for the same reason I am," he says, pacing the room. "He wants you to take the SAT and bring up the school's average. Am I right?"

"Probably."

"Good to know he and I are on the same page. Listen, I really can't stay—there's a campaign fund-raiser over at Chez Shea—but this shouldn't take long. You're obviously a very smart young man. I think Phillip must have gotten off on the wrong foot with you. He still has a lot to learn about people skills."

An odd movement in the hall catches Karl's eye. It's Lizette, outside the doorway, hiding from Upchurch, wiggling her thumb at Karl, sliding it horizontally, over and over, above her head. What could this mean? It looks like she wants him to set his hair on fire with a cigarette lighter.

The switch! He turned the mike off to save battery power and forgot to turn it back on.

"Excuse me a second," he tells Mr. Upchurch, and hurries with his IV pole into the bathroom, where he flushes the toilet, slides the switch, and readjusts his hair in the mirror.

"Sorry to interrupt," he says, and climbs back into the bed.

Mr. Upchurch turns his back to Karl. "You know why I'm here. Let's be frank."

"What? I can't hear you, my ears are a little clogged. Could you come closer?"

Karl is sweating all over, including his scalp. Will he electrocute himself? Not really: a nine-volt battery can't deliver a fatal shock. But he learned long ago in the garage that it can give you a painful burn—painful enough so he would have to tear the microphone off his scalp—which gives him all the more reason to sweat.

"Let's get down to it, Karl," Mr. Upchurch says, but—can't he understand English?—he's still facing the door, making sure no one else walks in.

"Hold on, wait, I wanted to ask you first"—*can't you just turn around?!*—"how do you know Mr. Klimchock? How come he got so upset when he saw you?"

Mr. Upchurch snorts to himself. "That's a long story. But I suppose it might help to share it with you." He paces the room as he speaks. "Klimmy and I went through school together, just like you and Phillip. Believe it or not, we had some things in common: good singing voices, and a strong interest in Felicia Maniscalco. His interest was more romantic, mine was purely physical. Our senior year, the class musical was *The King and I.* Everyone knew Felicia would play Anna—no one else could compare. That's why Klimmy and I both wanted to play the king: to get close to her. But, while Klimmy assumed his talent would win him the part—and he really did have a terrific voice, much better than mine—I wanted it more. I made an arrangement with the kid who was playing the piano during auditions. In exchange for an outrageous fee, he messed up while playing for Klimmy. Your Mr. Klimchock was a highstrung young man; the fumbling piano threw him completely off. He had a fit, right there on the auditorium stage, in front of Felicia and everyone else. It was sad to see." Upchurch smirks, still tickled by the memory. "So, I played the king, and he ended up playing Tuptim's secret boyfriend—the monk. I'll tell you something: bouncing around the stage with Felicia, singing 'Shall We Dance?' under the lights, that's still one of the best memories of my life."

An incredible thought distracts Karl: he sympathizes with Mr. Klimchock!

"Did you end up marrying her?" he asks.

"Are you joking? She was an airhead. Her talents were all anatomical."

At this moment, Karl's main concern is getting Upchurch to turn around and face the mike. But he's afraid of being too obvious. "I'm not sure I get the point of the story."

"I'll be blunt, then. I'm still the same guy, Karl. When I want something, I get it. That includes winning the mayoral race, and getting my son into Harvard."

Some inner instinct tells Karl that it might help to taunt Upchurch. Maybe then he'll get mad and spell out his demands without wasting more time.

"Why do you want to be mayor so badly? Are you a megalomaniac?"

Upchurch raises one eyebrow, surprised but not impressed. "No, it's not about power for power's sake. It's about what you can do with it. There are opportunities in this town that have gone to waste."

"Such as?"

"I can't go into specifics. But I'll say this much: after I'm elected, there'll be a lot more than ducks in Swivel Brook Park."

This is getting way off the subject, but—*Upchurch wants to build houses in the prettiest park in town?!*

"I see you're surprised. Don't worry, it'll be very tastefully done. How do you like the name Brookside?"

Nurse Francesca interrupts them with a cheerful "Hi, Karl." She's pushing a haggard man with a mustache in a wheelchair. The man's foot is thickly wrapped in bandages. "Say hello to your new roommate, Mister Prell. Or, excuse me, *Officer* Prell. He stopped a robbery at the TCBY today."

"It wasn't a robbery, it was a drunk waving a gun around," says Officer Prell unhappily. "I just wish I had bulletproof shoes."

As Nurse Francesca sets the policeman up in Mr. Hydine's old bed, Karl and his visitor share a scowl. They have important things to say, private things. How can they talk now? *(You had to blab about your real estate projects!)*

Karl's plan is ruined. He's stopped—defeated—destroyed.

Randall Upchurch, however, won't let a mere wounded cop foil his scheme. "Excuse us," he tells the nurse and her patient, "Karl wanted to tell me something in private."

He draws the curtain all the way around the bed and comes within six inches of Karl's nose. (Bless you, Nurse Francesca!) "No time for chitchat now," he whispers. "You're going to take the SAT Saturday. You'll transmit the answers to Phillip and the others. He told me about the scheme with the pencil—it's brilliant. I'll make it worth your while. Let's say, five thousand dollars cash, in two installments, one after the test and one after the scores come back."

"But what if I say no?"

"Then a pack of hungry dogs will enter your home while you sleep and leave nothing but three sets of bones."

"Um—literally or figuratively?" Karl asks.

Mr. Upchurch gives Karl a long, hard, contemptuous glare—an especially scary experience because of the microphone in his hair. A fresh torrent of sweat pours from him. The tension is too much. He twitches, and that sudden movement undoes the rubber cement's grip. He can feel the little black box slip a quarter-inch to the side.

"Hey, Karl," Nurse Francesca calls through the curtain, "in case I don't see you before you go home, good luck in school and everything."

"Thanks," he tells the curtain. "Am I going home soon?"

"Any time now."

Her footsteps fade away. They're going to discharge him before he gets Klimchock on tape. But it doesn't really matter, because Randall Upchurch will murder him when he sees the microphone fall off his head.

"I would take a shower first thing, if I were you," Upchurch tells him. "You sweat like a pig."

"Mm-hm," Karl replies.

"You won't let us down, right?"

"I'll be there."

"Good man. And just to make sure, I'll be listening from my car across the street."

That's it—he's gone. Karl has escaped the first of the swinging axes, but there's no time for celebration. He grabs the mike and speaks straight into it, whispering. "Lizette! Come! Emergency!"

"You're soaked!" she observes as she slips inside the curtain. "What'd he do, hose you down?"

He holds up the little mike. "The glue lost its grip. And they're going to send me home any minute now. I don't know what to do!"

Her father didn't leave the rubber cement, and even if he had, there's not enough time for it to dry.

Drowning in a sea of despair, banging his bones against the rocks of hysteria, Karl shakes his head and lets out a thin, high squeak.

"Stop it," Lizette commands. "Just calm down."

Since he can't stop shaking his head, she takes drastic action, grabbing him by the shoulders and *really* shaking him. His head flies around like a bobble-head doll's.

She keeps her grip on his shoulders even after she stops shaking him. For a moment or three, it looks as if she may crash through the invisible wall and kiss him—but then she lets go and takes the microphone from him. "Let's just get this done," she says.

Taking the Orbit gum out of her mouth, she flattens it against the dried rubber cement on the bottom of the microphone and sets it back on Karl's head, pushing painfully hard. Then she fluffs his damp hair around it. "You've looked better," she says, and hurries out.

She doesn't get far, though. "Excuse me," says a friendly old lady, just outside the curtain. "I'm looking for Karl Petrofsky. I have his discharge papers."

"I just saw him run into the toilet to throw up," Lizette replies. "He said something about the food here."

"Oh," says the pleasant lady.

"Maybe you should come back in a half hour or so," Lizette suggests.

"I'll do that. Could you tell him to have someone with him who can take him home?"

"I'll let him know. Soon as he stops heaving."

"Thank you."

Before Karl can fully comprehend his debt to Lizette, a hand yanks the curtain open.

"What was *he* doing here?" Mr. Klimchock whispers, red-faced.

"He? Nothing. Why?"

Klimchock goes to the doorway and checks the hall, then returns to Karl's bedside. "I'll ask again. What was *HE* doing here?"

The wormy vein appears on his forehead again.

"He just came to visit. He's a friend of my family—my mother. They know each other from work."

Klimchock regards Karl with distrust and distaste. "You're lying. Why would Randall Upchurch come visit you?"

His eyes move right and left, the outward signs of fevered thinking. He takes a whistling, inward breath.

"Phillip is in this with you! Isn't he?"

Klimchock's face lights up with glee. If he were a miser, there would be dollar signs on his eyeballs.

"It's too good to be true. Phillip Upchurch! Glory, glory, hallelujah!"

Karl has never seen the assistant principal this happy. Possibly, no one has. A small but heavy weight sits on his scalp, reminding him of his mission.

"What exactly do you want me to do, Mr. Klimchock?"

"I've already told you. This doesn't change the plan—it just means the prize will be bigger than I ever hoped."

"Could you just remind me of the details? I've been sick, I can't remember what you said."

Klimchock gazes at Karl questioningly. He pauses and listens through the curtain as visitors approach the doorway and pass. Then he comes closer, just as Upchurch did.

Unlike Randall Upchurch, though, Klimchock gropes Karl's chest through the flimsy blue hospital gown. His fingers probe every inch of flesh and bone.

"Hey!" Karl protests. "Stop that!"

"Are you wearing a wire, Karl? Is that it? Are you and Upchurch setting a trap?"

With the hidden microphone held in place only by a soft, malleable wad of gum, Karl states emphatically, "No! And get your hands off me—that's totally inappropriate."

Klimchock backs away. "Apologies. I suppose I'm overly suspicious."

While Klimchock blushes, a wave of confusion and discomfort breaks over Karl. *What am I doing?*—he can hear the question asked in his own voice, internally but loudly. Observing himself from above, he doesn't like what he sees. It's just . . . *sleazy*, trapping these two men. Nasty and merciless as they are, he doesn't want to be the sort of person who lies and schemes to destroy others. Yes, they deserve to be exposed, to be stopped—but look how devious he's being. The whole thing nauseates him.

Keeping his voice to a murmur, Klimchock begins again. "Can we finish our business now?"

A clamor interrupts him. "There he is!" "How's it going, Hopalong?" "What did the doctors say, will you ever tap-dance again?" "He needed this like he needs a hole in the foot."

The boisterous off-duty cops keep teasing Officer Prell—and as they do, Samantha comes storming into the room, rips open the curtain, and says, "I know what's going on! It's a conspiracy! You want Phillip to be the valedictorian! You're pressuring Karl to mess up on purpose, aren't you? Aren't you?!"

Before Mr. Klimchock can even process this accusation, Lizette is there, pulling on Samantha's arm. "You're crazy! Let them be."

"You're in cahoots with them!" Samantha accuses her.

"What kind of person are you? Nobody says *cahoots*."

"You're trying to shift the spotlight, but it won't work."

"Young lady," Mr. Klimchock says, "you've misread this entire situation. Believe me."

Samantha breaks free of Lizette 's grip. "I'll stand by you, Karl. Don't let them intimidate you. You're Number One!"

Karl's heart hasn't beat for several seconds, at least that he's aware of. He pleads with her. "They're not pressuring me! Just go out there and sit on the bench—everything's okay!"

"I'm not leaving until they do."

"*Please* go!"

Samantha shakes her head. "You've got him terrorized. I'm warning you two—if you try to cheat Karl out of his rightful place, I swear, I'll get the story on CNN."

"Would you just *leave*?" Lizette says.

"Hello, Mister Petrofsky, are you feeling better now?"

The sweet little old lady with the clipboard is back.

"I just need you to sign these papers for me. I'll bet you're happy to be going home."

None of the four of them says a word. One of the cops calls through the curtain, "Everything okay in there?"

A gurgling comes from deep in Karl's gut. He squeezes his eyes shut, fighting down his rising gorge. "Karl?" Lizette asks. "What's going on?"

"Could someone bring me a garbage can?"

Lizette, mistaking Karl's illness for an Oscar-worthy performance, says, "Mr. Klimchock, will you stay with Karl while I go get a nurse?"

"Of course. The rest of you had better wait outside."

"I think," the lady with the clipboard says, "we'd better wait a bit longer before discharging you."

When Karl opens his eyes again, he's alone with Mr. Klimchock, surrounded by the drawn curtain. "Well done," Mr. Klimchock says. "Now let's finish our conversation before the earth quakes and swallows the entire hospital." He drops his voice to a whisper. "You have to take the SAT, Karl. You have to cheat again, so I can catch the rest of them. You don't have a choice. I've already offered to keep your cheating out of your school records *and* to lie to colleges that you're a top-notch fencer. You can't say no. Think of your parents. I'm sure it would kill them to see your academic career snuffed out before it began."

That's it: Karl is done. He has caught Klimchock in his trap.

"All right," he says gloomily. "I'll do it."

Mr. Klimchock glows. Then he bursts into song—quietly, so the off-duty cops won't hear, but still in a pure and handsome tenor. "Wonder of wonder, miracle of miracles . . ."

Armed with the evidence to crush Klimchock and Upchurch, both of whom would cheerfully crush him, Karl doesn't rejoice. Far from it. After all this frantic effort, he would like nothing better than to throw the recordings in the trash. He's just not the Enemy-Devouring Type; the whole plan disturbs him more and more with each passing moment.

In this state of nausea, he remembers what Lizette said: *I wish there were a way for Karl to duck and let them fire away at each other.*

Karl wishes there were, too.

Midnight. A ringing noise pokes into Karl's sleep, annoyingly, persistently.

His cell phone.

Eyes still closed, "Hello?"

"Karl, right?"

The voice belongs to a guy about his age, but Karl doesn't recognize it. "Who's this?"

"You can call me the Guru. I'm the master of deceit, the specialist in scams and schemes, the world's champion cheater. A girl named Cara got in touch with me—she said you got caught, and now you're planning to sacrifice yourself so you can bring down some tyrannical assistant principal. Do I have the facts right?"

Down the hall, at the nurses' station, a radio is playing softly. In less than a minute, the guy on the phone has shown himself to be possibly the most obnoxious person Karl has ever listened to.

"It's a little more complicated than that, but basically, yeah, that's right."

"Okay. Free advice: don't let so-called Nobility fog up your brain. There has to be a better way—but you won't find it till you expand your thinking."

"All I've been *doing* is thinking. I can't see any other way."

"That's why I'm here, kid. I'm your crisis hotline, your guardian angel, your personal mahatma. You've got to stop letting them intimidate you."

The Guru's chattering leaves Karl deeply skeptical. *This guy is having way too much fun.* He doubts that the self-proclaimed authority will have a single good suggestion to make.

"If you've got any ideas, would you please just tell me?"

"Hey, I can't solve your problems for you. All I can do is open your mind and lead you to the Gates of Wisdom. You have to go the rest of the way yourself."

If he doesn't say something useful in the next thirty seconds, Karl resolves, *I'm hanging up.*

"Go ahead, Guru. I'm listening."

In the empty air on the other end, Karl hears the sound of a mouse clicking in rapid bursts. While he's supposedly saving Karl from doom, the great Guru is also playing a game on his computer. Wonderful.

"Okay. First we eliminate self-destruction as an option. Then we think: how can we scare the living crap out of this guy so he'll leave you alone? I'm not talking about illegal weaponry here. More like butterflies with huge eyes on their wings—give the illusion of great size and menace. What could you say to this fiend that would . . ."

The rest of the Guru's blather evaporates into the air, a harmless, odorless gas. He has said the magic words; he has given Karl the answer, without realizing it. Despite the emptiness of his boasts, he was right about one thing: there *is* another way out.

Karl hangs up and takes the pen and the hospital notepad from the bedside table. He's got a great deal of planning to do. Between now and the SAT, he may not have time to sleep.

Chapter 15

Early morning fog. Damp chill in the air. Quiet out, except for a blue jay shrieking and the loose fan belt slapping as Mom lets the engine idle.

Karl's heavy exhaustion helps subdue his anxiety. Ironic: for once, he's nervous before a test like everyone else, though for very different reasons.

"You're sure you're up to this?" his mother asks. "You don't have to go in. You can take it the next time instead."

In his altered state, he notices every crumpled scrap of paper in the cup holder, and the coffee stain on the emergency-brake handle. "I'm totally fine," he claims. A little burp brings up the taste of the hard-boiled eggs she served him an hour before.

"Quick: *antelope* is to *deer* as *cantaloupe* is to what?"

"Mom, they don't give analogies anymore."

His head is light as he steps out of the car, though his body seems to have put on an extra hundred pounds. He moves slowly so he won't lose his balance and fall over.

"I'll pick you up at twelve-thirty," his mother calls through the open window. "Hopefully the car'll be fixed by then. If not, we'll have a nice walk home. Don't forget to eat those nuts in the break! I love you."

He blows her a kiss—their old habit, an involuntary reflex—and the white Accord heads down the street.

He walks along the ragged line outside the school door. Antonio Feferman sips casually from a Starbucks cup; Ivan Fretz turns the pages of a thick review book, skimming with rapid head movements. The sleeves of Karl's jacket rub his arm hairs uncomfortably; that's how he knows he's still sick.

"Who let the cadaver out of the lab?"

Lizette pulls Karl into the line.

"Hey, Karl, you don't look your usual bubbly self."

That's Matt, nervously nodding. Jonah's there, too. Subdued, he shakes Karl's hand.

"So," Karl says softly, "you're taking the test even though . . ."

"I'm hoping they'll let me back into school. *Some*how."

He smiles, trying to be brave. There's something different about him. He looks more grown up, less awkward.

"Braces off. Last week."

"You've been out of touch, big guy."

"Yeah, you missed my three home-run game," Lizette says.

She seems tense—which is understandable on SAT

day, especially since she's involved in a conspiracy, and also doesn't know exactly where she stands with Karl and whether they'll soon be a couple or will stay—sigh—just friends.

"So, old chum," says Matt, "would you be open to sending us the right answers, telepathically?"

"Look at him," Lizette comments, a quick change of subject. "He's a wreck. You better hope the essay topic is Why I Feel Like Dog Doo Today."

"You wouldn't be nervous, would you, Karl?" Matt pokes him in the chest. "That would not be logical."

He deserves the taunts, he supposes. After all, he did heartlessly abandon the three of them. The funny thing is, he *enjoys* the teasing. It's good to be back.

Farther back on the line, a slender patch of blue moves metronome-fashion in the air. This is Blaine's sweater sleeve, waving. Behind him stand Vijay, Ian, Tim, and Noah. Vijay sends Karl a discreet thumbs-up.

Karl turns his head away, as if dodging a blinding flash.

Up at the head of the line, Phillip Upchurch stands apart in his khaki slacks and blazer. (If a Harvard scout puts in a surprise appearance, at least Phillip won't have to worry about being underdressed.) Mr. Sweddy, the gym teacher, checks his watch repeatedly. With him stand four unfamiliar men in dark suits and sunglasses. Each has a square white badge on his jacket, but they're too far away to read the little words. "Who do you think they are?" Karl asks.

Lizette: "FBI?"

"They look more like an a cappella group," says Matt.

Eight o'clock. The line begins to move. Karl pats his pockets: three number two pencils in his windbreaker's inside pocket (all wooden, none electronic); admission ticket in his windbreaker's outer pocket, left side; student ID in left pants pocket; Baggie full of salted nuts in windbreaker's outer pocket, right side; iPod Nano loaded with incriminating recordings in left shirt pocket, covered by flap; and digital transmitter in right shirt pocket, likewise hidden by flap.

"Into the mouth of the monster marched the innocent multitudes," Matt moans.

Passing through the entranceway, Karl reads the badges of the men in dark suits. They all say the same thing: ETS, PRINCETON.

Educational Testing Service. The makers of the test.

What's that thumping in the distance? Oh—his heart.

The students file through the dim hallway, past the band room, the office, the nurse's office, the auditorium, the art studio—around many corners, like obedient mice in a maze. The school looks different this Saturday morning, with all the doors closed and the room lights out. Bleak. Deserted.

In the gym, four teachers—Watney, Singh, Franklin, and Verp—huddle together by the bleachers.

Karl and his friends mill around like everyone else, waiting for whatever comes next. "Now I know how cattle feel when they're herded into the slaughterhouse," Jonah says.

"Son, you've got to work on that attitude," Lizette replies.

Karl's laugh dies fast when he notices the entire Confederacy hovering just behind him—including Phillip Upchurch.

"Hey, amigo," says Blaine. "Good to go?"

Though Karl has engineered a massive deception, a simple lie is harder to pull off. "Rmff," he says, nodding.

Blaine pats him on the back. "Good luck—to all of us." He adds a private murmur: "Visualize success."

"Attention, students," Miss Verp announces, in a voice like a drawer full of silverware landing on the floor. "You will now divide yourselves into four equal groups."

The teachers spread out along the bottom row of the bleachers and wait for the students to line up in front of them. Karl wanders over to Herr Franklin, who seems the least likely of the four to notice anything. His friends come with him, and so does the Confederacy.

The mass migration arouses suspicion. Here comes Miss Verp, whispering in Herr Franklin's ear—and there he goes, taking over her group. Alarmingly, Miss Verp gives Karl a malicious smile as she says, "Follow me, students."

Something pink hurries into the gym. It's Samantha, wearing a satin jacket with padded shoulders, searching urgently among the students as they file out the opposite way.

Karl turns to hide, but it's too late, she's spotted him. "We got stuck in the car, waiting for the Healthy Hearts Walk-athon to cross Jefferson Avenue. You never saw a bunch of people move so slowly."

"Ssh!" Miss Verp hisses, and points wrathfully at Samantha.

Each of the four teachers leads his or her group a different way. By the time the Verp group arrives at room 211, one of the ETS men is already there, standing guard with crossed arms over two plastic bags on the teacher's desk.

The students fan out and take seats—Samantha and Lizette flank Karl, eyeing each other with suspicion and hostility, respectively—but Miss Verp corrects them. "Don't sit directly behind or next to anyone else. Leave at least one empty seat in front, back, left, and right. No one should be within four feet of anyone else."

After some comical shuffling about (if only he could laugh!), Karl ends up in the middle of the room, with Samantha in front of him to the left and Lizette behind him to the right. Miss Verp hands a test booklet to each student individually—she tosses Karl's on his desk, *slap*—and then repeats the process with the answer sheets.

"Before we begin filling in the forms and reading the instructions, let me introduce Mr. O'Malley."

The man in the suit, who has stationed himself at the back of the room, salutes with three fingers and a microscopic smile as the students turn and gaze at him. He has a pasty, blotchy complexion, a sturdy physique, and very small ears.

"Mr. O'Malley is here on official business from the ETS in Princeton. I can't say more, but I'd advise you to follow all of the directions to the letter, and keep your eyes on your own work."

"I called them," Samantha whispers to Karl. "They have a hotline for tips."

"Ssh!"

While Miss Verp writes the school's address and code number on the blackboard, the members of the Confederacy trade glances that express defiance, smug confidence, boredom, and amusement. Vijay and Blaine check in with

Karl silently: Vijay with a *No sweat* wink, and Blaine with a questioning look, *You okay?*

Not only is Karl not okay, he has begun (despite Vijay's wink) to sweat profusely. If Mr. O'Malley sees him activate the iPod and transmitter, his plans will come flying apart like pieces of a giant turbine hit by a grenade, with lethal results.

Miss Verp reads the detailed instructions in a loud, buzzing monotone, pausing every minute or so to look up and ask, "Does everyone understand?" but not waiting for a reply. Acidic fluids have been sloshing in Karl's stomach all morning. Imagining Mr. O'Malley leading him out of the room in handcuffs, he yearns to glance back at Lizette for moral support; he can't afford to attract the ETS man's attention, though.

Woozy, dizzy, fuzzy-brained, he remembers his adversaries, Klimchock and Upchurch, and pictures them playing soccer with his head. Frankly, he can't visualize success.

Despite what Karl might think, Mr. Klimchock is not laughing nefariously at this moment, or rubbing his hands together in an archvillainous manner. He's standing in his office with a helmetlike headset on: a device he read about in *High School Administration Quarterly*. Developed for precisely this purpose by a physics teacher in Bowbells, North Dakota, the headset makes radio waves visible. Mr. Klimchock tunes his clock-radio to the local oldies station, turns around, and sees his office filled with rippling curtains of sound. In bliss, he floats through this aurora borealis of luminous, ghostly filaments, and anticipates victory.

He turns to the clock-radio again and sees a glowing,

throbbing circle that indicates the speaker. The vibrating diaphragm in each cheater's earphone will show up this same way, minutes from now, when he leaves his office and visits the four classrooms.

His quest has succeeded, at last.

Across the street from the school, a single car is parked, a silver Mercedes in the shade of a locust tree. Inside, Randall Upchurch has his radio tuned to quiet static on 98.5 FM as he reviews the talking points for his speech at the Chamber of Commerce lunch, later today. This is a pleasant time for him: his campaign manager has drafted some excellent material (he especially likes the bit about better schools with smarter—i.e., less—spending), and he's enjoying the knowledge that he has gone the extra mile for his son, taking time from his impossibly busy schedule to make sure the Petrofsky kid keeps his word, because this day will be crucial in shaping Phillip's future. (Too bad his son has grown up to be such a—well, never mind that, he's still young, he may grow out of it.)

The clock in room 211 reads 8:44. Miss Verp finished reading the instructions five minutes ago and has let the students savor the moments before the test in pure, nerve-racking silence.

Ivan Fretz—that dismal, crushed creature—whispers over his shoulder, "Good luck, Karl."

"Thanks. You too."

Ivan rolls his eyes and sighs grimly, as if to say, *It doesn't matter how I do, I'm doomed no matter what.*

Miss Verp goes to the door and closes it quietly. "Begin section one!" she screeches.

Mr. O'Malley moves up and down the aisles, inspecting. The Confederates pretend to read their test booklets while waiting for the answers to reach their earphones. Samantha searches the room like a hungry raptor, paying special attention to Blaine.

Karl sees his chance: a moment will come, and it may come only once, when Mr. O'Malley will have his back to Karl as he approaches the front of the room, and his body will obstruct Miss Verp's line of sight. Karl will have less than a second. He must not fumble.

Unexpectedly calm, he awaits the Verpal eclipse. When it comes, he pushes on each shirt pocket once, barely perceptibly, activating first the transmitter, then the iPod.

That's all it takes. As he starts work on the first section of the test, the two devices deliver the following message to all who happen to be tuned to 98.5 megahertz:

"This is Karl Petrofsky. Certain students asked me to help them cheat on the SAT. Mr. Klimchock found out and tried to get me to go ahead and cheat, so he could track the signal and see which students were listening. (If you can hear this, you may want to take out your earphones and hide them, fast.) Phillip Upchurch's father also wanted me to cheat, for different reasons. Can I prove any of this? Yes."

Next, the listeners hear Mr. Klimchock say, "You have to take the SAT, Karl. You have to cheat again, so I can catch the rest of them. You don't have a choice. I've already offered to keep your cheating out of your school records *and* to lie to colleges that you're a top-notch fencer. You can't say no."

A plasticky snap (the sound of Lizette's tape recorder button) separates Klimchock's voice from Upchurch's.

"No time for chitchat now. You're going to take the SAT Saturday. You'll transmit the answers to Phillip and the others. He told me about the scheme with the pencil—it's brilliant. I'll make it worth your while. Let's say, five thousand dollars cash, in two installments, one after the test and one after the scores come back."

Karl's voice returns now. "Only a few people know about this. I could have sent the tapes to all the newspapers, but I decided to give you both a chance. *Leave me alone.* Stop tyrannizing the school, Mr. Klimchock—and take that note off my student record. Mr. Upchurch, stop threatening me, and leave Swivel Brook Park alone. Because I can still mail the tapes. And don't try to steal them, because I've left copies in secret locations, addressed to the *New York Times,* the *Star Ledger,* and *New Jersey Magazine.* If anything happens to me, they go straight in the mailbox. This concludes the audio portion of our broadcast."

Although Karl managed to read his prepared speech with quiet bravado, he's in a different state of mind now. Keeping his head down, he struggles to concentrate on sentence completion questions as Mr. O'Malley moves slowly up and down the aisles. And Mr. O'Malley is just one of his fears. What if the angry Confederates stab him with their pencils? Or maybe Mr. Klimchock will run into the room and skewer him with a sword. Or, Randall Upchurch may bash him in the skull with a solid gold brick.

Of course, there's also a chance that the technology failed, and the recording didn't reach any of them—in which case, as soon as the test is over, Blaine and the others will tear him limb from limb.

No—that's one worry he can cross out, because up in the front row, Blaine is taking off his sweater. Mr. Cool has suddenly gotten hot; sweaty gray patches have formed on the armpits of his polo shirt. The sweater removal has mussed his hair, a first.

Over by the windows, Ian is breathing hard and fast.

Back to the test Karl goes, hunching over the desk, shutting out everything and everyone—and therefore not noticing Samantha, who's staring back at the little red light in his shirt pocket, which is visible because the pocket flap has popped up the way those flaps so often do. The short antenna is standing up, diagonally, just enough to make its function clear.

Samantha can't figure out what this means—until she does. Her eyes open wide; the mascaraed lashes look like hair standing on end. This could go a few different ways—hurt, horror, disillusionment. She draws a colossal breath—her chest inflates to twice its normal size. With the cumulative rage of a woman long deceived but not any more, she prepares to blast her trumpet to the world, *Karl Petrofsky is cheating!*

A pasty hand in a dark sleeve grips her padded pink shoulder. "Young lady, come with me, please."

Mr. O'Malley has levitated her from her seat. "Take your things," he tells her, and confiscates her test book and answer sheet.

"I saw someone cheating," she blares.

"Must have been your own reflection," he replies. "You've

been looking everywhere but at your own test the whole time."

"I'm a reporter! I've been investigating them for months! I'm the one who tipped you guys off!"

"Ma'am," Mr. O'Malley tells Miss Verp, "please destroy this test book and answer sheet. She's done for today."

"You can't do this! I'm not leaving."

"You're interfering with all of these people's test taking. If you don't walk out that door right now, I'll have to invalidate the test for everyone here. And you'll have to answer to them for their wasted time and mental anguish."

"Look in his shirt pocket! Just look!"

Her frenzied insistence perplexes Mr. O'Malley—but not Miss Verp, who strides eagerly down the aisle and sends her cold, stubby fingertips into Karl's shirt pockets, right and left. Good thing he slipped the iPod and transmitter into his pants pocket as soon as Samantha opened her mouth.

"I'm not the one who cheated!" Samantha bellows as the door closes behind her.

"Hm!" Miss Verp comments: *you may have hidden the evidence, Petrofsky, but I know you're in this up to your skinny neck.*

She returns to her desk without further probing, however, leaving Karl and the other students to puzzle their way through the long test—separately and honestly.

12. *Ms. Newcastle disliked Arnold's ____ manner; she much preferred his brother's ____.*

    a. *felonious...belligerence*

b. *gullible…decrepitude*

c. *naïve…ostentation*

d. *devious…simplicity*

e. *loquacious…tenacity*

While Karl and the other students were acting out this drama in room 211, a very different scene unfolded nearby.

Giddy with anticipation, unable to sit still, Mr. Klimchock roamed the halls for many minutes, floating in a substance-less web of radio waves. At 8:45, test time, he climbed the stairs to the second floor. His headphones picked up the first signal, a crackly snap, just as he entered room 223. "This is Karl Petrofsky," said a familiar voice.

He stopped in the doorway. This wasn't what they agreed—

No need to dwell on his rage and panic. Let's fast-forward to the end of the recording, which finds him still in the doorway, watched curiously by Mr. Watney, a pudgy ETS man, and a room full of students.

Choosing a course of action comes easily, instinctively. He flees.

Face on fire, *exposed,* he stops at his office to gather his theater posters, personal files, and Les Miz mug. Then he heads for the teachers' parking lot, where the boxlike black Scion awaits him in the space labeled ASS ANT P IN PAL.

After shoving his belongings into the rear, he backs out and zips away—but brakes as he leaves the lot, because there, across the street from the school, is Randall Upchurch, swinging a tennis racquet with two hands, furiously clanging it against a streetlight like a psychotic lumberjack. To Mr. Klimchock, this odd scene represents a faint ray of light amid the darkness of disgrace. He lowers his window as he drives by and laughs at his old enemy—or, shouts, really, "HA!"

The morning passes quickly for Karl; his concentration carries him through the hours until Miss Verp collects the answer sheets and test books. She counts them under Mr. O'Malley's watchful eye, checks each book to make sure the test taker's name is on it, and then the students are free to go.

Lizette taps Karl lightly on the head. "Success?"

He surveys the room cautiously. Blaine, Vijay, Noah, Ian, and Tim are filing out with the others. Not one of them glances back at Karl.

"I think so."

Matt has stuck two pencils in his nostrils, eraser-end up, and they bounce against his lips as he speaks: "That was fun, let's do it again."

"Was Lois the victim of *calumny* or *obfuscation?*" asks Jonah.

"I don't even remember that one," Karl says.

Like blood returning to a sleeping foot, optimism seeps back into his spirit. Maybe his plan actually worked. Maybe he can live a normal life again.

"So, how'dja do?" Lizette asks as they exit the classroom.

"Okay, I think. How about you?"

"Same as you. Minus a few hundred points."

The hallway has already emptied out. No one lies in wait for him. No rifles point at his head.

"I just want to go to sleep for three days," Karl mumbles.

"Nobody's stopping you."

Lizette's teasing is ambiguous: testy or fond? He remembers that *she cares about him so much.* The test is over; time to deal with that Other Thing.

The walk down the stairs lasts a long time, because he's anxiously wondering whether Lizette wants him to hold her hand. No matter what she wants, he can't do it—not in front of Jonah and Matt.

"Talk to you a minute, Karl?"

They're at the school's front door, about to exit. Blaine is standing off to the side. He's got his blue sweater on again, and he's not smiling. "In private, if you don't mind."

Lizette whispers, "I'll wait right outside."

The Slightly Irregular Three leave the building.

"That was an interesting surprise," Blaine says.

Unsure what form the assault will take—words or blows— Karl leans backward, away from the reach of Blaine's fists.

"You don't mess around. *Envelopes in secret locations.* That's heavy-duty."

Karl has a strong impulse to confess that he exaggerated, that there's really only one envelope, at his aunt's house in Teaneck.

"I just want to say one thing," Blaine begins.

"Look—I was in an impossible position."

"Just one thing," Blaine insists. "Thank you. For keeping us out of Klimchock's trap."

He offers Karl his hand. As they shake, he sighs. "Looks like I'll be going to Princeton—Review, that is."

He pats Karl on the back and pushes the heavy door open. "Adios, amigo. I'll talk to you in a few years, with an investment opportunity."

The door closes between them. Karl slumps against the handrail, exhausted.

Someone thumps on the door, *wham wham wham wham wham*.

"Karl? You okay in there?"

He pushes the lock bar to let Lizette in, but she pulls the door open so fast that he stumbles out into the bright sunlight.

He sees the near future with perfect clarity: he will tumble down the concrete steps, all dignity gone, and Lizette will lose her respect for him. He may lose a tooth or two as well.

That's not how the scene plays out, though. She grabs his arm before he takes the tumble, and hoists him up almost vertical.

"Elegant move," she comments.

Regaining his balance, with Lizette's hand in his, he blinks in the sunlight. A peaceful breeze stirs the new leaves on the trees. There are no teachers or students around, just him and Lizette.

"Looks like you climbed out of that hole you were in," she says. "Congratulations."

You couldn't choreograph a better lead-in to a first kiss if you planned for months. In fact, Karl knows, if he *doesn't* kiss her, he'll be a fool, a coward, a jerk.

Nevertheless . . .

"What is it, Karl?"

Nothing he can put into words. Just that he's scared out of his wits.

Honk!

"Anybody need a ride?" his mother calls from the car.

RULE #16: In any given situation, most people take the easy way out. Sure, I could stop cheating, stop taking risks, spare myself the penalties, make everything simple: graduate on time instead of having to repeat the year, go to a prestigious college, get a high-paying job, get an attractive wife and perfect kids. But that would mean Death by Boredom. Let others play life straight. I choose cheating!

Chapter 16

The ropes are cutting into Karl's hands and wrists. He should have put on work gloves, but it's too late now, he's got the Turtle in the air and it's swinging like a heavy pendulum, something he didn't anticipate—and another problem, the beam he slung the rope over is just a single two-by-four, and it's creaking under the weight. All he can do now is hurry and lower the Turtle into the test vat (a round kiddy pool, four inflated rings decorated with happy goldfish) as fast as possible, before the garage roof comes crashing down—except, he has to wait for the Turtle to stop swinging, or it'll hit the topmost ring of the pool, burst it, and flood the garage floor.

A stranger stops at the open garage door. The man is so quiet, Karl doesn't realize he's there until he asks, "Karl Petrofsky?"

The visitor is a thin, white-haired man in a brown suit and yellow bow tie, with gold-rimmed glasses and pale, softly wrinkled skin. The face is vaguely familiar; Karl has seen this man before, though he can't remember where.

There's no way to hide the Turtle this time. "Yes?"

"May I come in?"

"I'm kind of busy right now."

The wooden beam groans overhead. Karl lowers the Turtle to within a few inches of the water's surface. The pendulum motion has narrowed; timing the drop carefully, he lets the rope slip through his hands. The Turtle raises a wave as it cuts into the water and gently pokes the inflated wall. Settling to the bottom, it leaves only a smooth steel dome showing above the surface.

"Is that for school?" the stranger asks. His voice is mild, and dry as paper.

"No, it's just something I made. Excuse me, I have to do something."

He bends over the kiddy pool and searches for air bubbles. There shouldn't be any. *Please, let there not be any*, he prays.

No bubbles surface. Yay!

"What does it do?" the stranger asks.

"Um—nothing. It's an art project."

"Oh. I see."

The visitor's wrinkled forehead shows that he doubts Karl's words. He seems concerned, as if the Turtle might be a weapon of mass destruction.

"I was just testing to see if it's watertight."

"Ah."

Karl leads his guest out of the garage and closes the door behind them. "Are you looking for my parents?"

"No. Don't you know who I am?"

"Should I?"

"Perhaps not. My name is Francis Hightower."

The principal! *That's* where Karl has seen him—leaving the school at the end of the day. Quietly. Anonymously.

Terror catches up with him like a bullet. He took the SAT a week ago; he thought he'd escaped without a scratch. It's never that easy, though, is it?

"Is something wrong?" he asks weakly.

"Wrong? No, I just came to thank you."

They're standing in the driveway. Mr. Hightower's shoe is practically touching the dirty red Frisbee that has sat under the forsythia hedge for the past six years.

"Um—thank me for what?"

Before Mr. Hightower can reply, Ivan Fretz waves to Karl from the sidewalk. He's walking his shaggy black dog. "How's it going, neighbor?"

For the first time since childhood, Ivan comes down the driveway. "Sorry to interrupt. I just wanted to run something by you. What would you think about making some extra money over the summer, tutoring me for the SAT?"

The dog sniffs his way up Karl's thigh.

"You're going to take it again?"

"I hardly even studied! It didn't seem to matter. But now it does, so—think it over, Karl. This could be good for both of us. Come on, Bibsy."

Ivan gives the leash a tug, and the dog growls as they go back the way they came.

"He seems cheerful," Mr. Hightower says.

"He had something really bad in his records, and it got taken off."

"I know that, Karl. I'm the one who took it off."

"Oh."

"As I said, I wanted to thank you. You accomplished what I wanted to do and couldn't for many years."

The sun of understanding begins to peek over the hills now, shedding its light on what was dark and mysterious.

"I'm not a public sort of person. I used to teach biology, and I enjoyed my work—but my wife felt that I should keep moving ahead, and so forth. The point is, I shouldn't have become a principal. When Mr. Klimchock offered to take over some of my more public duties, I gladly accepted. But that turned out to be unwise, as you know. I've been searching for a way to get rid of him for years. I don't know how to thank you."

Cautiously, in case this is some sort of trap, Karl asks, "Why do you think I had anything to do with him leaving?"

The principal looks down at the red Frisbee, away from Karl. "When the technician was installing those hidden cameras, I had him put one in Mr. Klimchock's office, too. I saw and heard what he said to you. If I'd had the power to fire him, I would have—but those cameras don't record, so I didn't have a strong enough case against him."

Hidden cameras! Of course! That Karl never guessed Klimchock's method only proves what a dolt a supposedly smart person can be.

But wait. The principal knew what Mr. Klimchock was

doing to Karl and never helped? He just hid in his office the whole time and let Karl fend for himself?

"You have every right to be angry at me—but I didn't want to ruin your future. If I'd gone to the superintendent, that would have left you with a terrible stain on your record. In the end, whatever you did had a much better outcome. What did you do, exactly? I still don't know."

Karl hesitates, still not sure he should trust Mr. Hightower.

"That's all right, Karl. Whatever it was, I salute you— because now I can go back to teaching biology until I retire, and I won't have to worry that the school will fall into a maniac's hands."

Shyly, the principal shakes Karl's hand. He smells very clean, in an old-fashioned way, like a bar of soap from a bygone era.

"You have my admiration, and my sincere apologies. I wish I could have helped you more."

"So do I. But I'm okay now."

The principal takes his leave. The brown suit passes the Fretz house, the Santangelos, the Carneys, and turns the corner. There's something extremely unusual about this man, but Karl can't put his finger on it.

Or—yes, he can. Mr. Hightower came here on foot.

An odd person. But probably a good biology teacher. Karl hopes so, anyway.

When he calls to invite Lizette to Swivel Brook Park, she answers, "Why?"

The tone is key here. *Why?* can be a straightforward question, but more often it's a challenge: *what you just said doesn't make sense, so you'd better give me a good reason (and I don't think you can).*

Lizette's *Why* has more teasing than insult in it. This is how it's been between them since that stumble at the school's front door. She has given up on him ever kissing her, it seems. Instead of waiting and hoping, or doing the kissing herself, she makes fun of him.

"There's something I want to show you," he replies.

"In the park, in the dark? Doesn't sound like something my daddy would approve of."

"Will you please just come with me?"

"I guess. I can't say no to you."

She picks him up after dinner, in her father's station wagon. She's wearing a Rutgers football jersey and her old Devil Rays cap, and the car has a chaotic pile of sporting goods in the back. Karl makes another of his resolutions on the way to the park: if the Turtle works, and she appreciates it—if she says something like, *Karl, this is amazing*—then he'll kiss her right then and there. No more fear and hesitation. Just a kiss, period.

On the other hand, the likelihood of her praising him is about equal to the chance that green kangaroos will rain down from the sky.

He takes her through the wooden playground fortress where he once found a plastic space shuttle, his first memory. The sky is a pale, post-sunset blue; the trees are silhouettes. "You're a mysterious person, Karl," Lizette says.

"Mmph," he replies.

The gravel path leads them to the stream. Karl takes a seat on a bench under a lamppost, and she joins him. Some old guys with bats and mitts laugh as they leave the dark softball field.

Karl gazes at the flowing water, trying to influence Lizette to do the same. He's waiting for her to notice what he brought her here to see, but she's too preoccupied. Staring at her lap, she shakes her head and snorts unhappily.

"What did you want to show me?" she asks finally.

"You have to look at the water."

She sees nothing unusual at first, just some ducks, tall grass, cattails, a couple of boulders. Farther downstream, the little waterfall makes a peaceful rushing sound.

Hold on, though.

One of the boulders in front of them isn't gray-black but shiny blue, a reflection of the sky. There are small holes, regularly spaced, drilled into the smooth surface. A nubby black thing pops up on top.

"Is that the thing you were building in your garage?"

"Uh-huh."

He reaches into his jacket and takes out a universal remote, the kind that can operate a TV, DVD player, and audio system. The buttons and their labels have all been painted black, except four: the Power button and three others, marked with little white symbols that Lizette interprets as a music note, a drop of water, and a complicated fishhook, upside down. (Or maybe it's a very sparse tree, a sapling with droopy branches.)

"Go ahead," Karl says, holding out the remote to her. "Turn it on."

"It's not gonna blow up the park, is it?"

"Probably not."

She hesitates. "You should do it yourself. Since it's the first time."

"I'd like you to."

She bends her head, and the visor of her cap covers her face—or, it would if Karl were in front of her. Even in the dim light, he can see that her cheek has turned red.

Accepting the remote, she says, "Here goes I don't know what," and presses Power.

Nothing happens.

"How do you know when it starts working?"

"You have to push the next button."

"Oh. I thought it was a dud."

She presses the button with the music note above it. A queer noise joins the quiet burble of the stream: a tremulous, flutelike hum. A moment later, the pulsating note deepens to a lower pitch—and then jumps to a higher one. The notes seem to change at random, but they all sound good.

"It's the scale Debussy used in *La Mer*," Karl explains. "The notes are all a whole tone apart."

"You're so bizarre, Karl."

These are not the words he was hoping to hear.

"Press the next button."

Expecting something water related—the little symbol is a droplet, after all—Lizette literally jumps off the bench when twenty thumb-size flames shoot from the metallic dome—bursting up and then shutting off, in the same rhythm as the musical notes.

"This is supposed to be a *flame*? It looks like a drop of water."

They watch the jets of fire and listen to the music. Karl worries intensely that Lizette thinks his creation is stupid.

"Should I press the last button?"

"Go ahead."

Expecting mechanical fish to leap from the water—why else the fishhook symbol?—she's taken by surprise when several fine streams of water spray from the dome. Each arc begins below the flames and travels away from the dome, so the falling drops won't put out the fire.

The symbol is a fountain, Lizette sees now—not an upside-down hook.

The yellow flames lend their color to the falling drops, turning them into moving necklaces of gold.

"So, is this what's supposed to happen?"

"Pretty much."

She watches the Turtle perform, torturing him by saying nothing. It was a mistake to bring her here, he decides. If she mocks his work, he won't even be able to talk to her anymore, let alone kiss her.

"Are you allowed to tell me how it does all that? Or is it like a magic trick?"

"Most of the power comes from the current of the stream. And I used the basic mechanism of a vibraphone to give it that trembly sound. It's hard to explain the machinery in words—but I can show you my sketches later if you want."

She nods, taking in the sound and light. He dares to hope.

"If only," she says, "you would use your genius for good and not evil."

It's a joke, not an insult—but you can't call it admiration, either. He's confused. Does she respect him, or does she think he's a dork?

The Turtle plays a haunting, random melody. The little flames bend in the breeze. A mallard paddles up to watch the fountain drops patter on the brook, and returns to report to his friends and family. Karl almost comments on this— *That must be where they got the name "Peeking Duck"*—but decides not to break the silence.

Lizette lets the air out of her lungs, an extended sigh.

How long can two teenagers writhe in their separate turmoil before one of them explodes—or lets fly a tension-breaking comment like that duck pun? Pretty long, I'd say— but we're not going to find out tonight, because an outside force intervenes, and that force's name is Cara.

She has cut her hair to finger-length and thinned her bangs into parallel lines with her forehead showing through. "Wow," she says, watching the Turtle perform. "So I guess it's not a spy submarine after all."

There's room for her to sit next to Karl, but she stays on her feet.

"Is this how you spend your free time?" Lizette asks. "Wandering around here after dark?"

"Karl asked me to come."

The hurt and confusion on Lizette's face (glimpsed briefly, before she covers up) make Karl yearn to reassure her.

"I invited a few friends," he explains. "It's like a premiere."

"So, I'll be back at school next week," Cara says.

"Really? That's great! Did the principal call you?"

"No, his secretary."

The Turtle toots, sonorously.

"Anyway, I can't stay—but it's good to see you two together. How's that going?"

No answer from the Tortured Twosome, except some strangled proto-noises.

"Okayyyyyy. Well, good luck. Excellent science project, Karl."

Her boots crunch away on the gravel. A car door opens and closes. Engine on, then fading into the distance.

You'd think the Turtle were the most fascinating object on earth: they can't take their eyes off it.

In the end, it's Lizette, not our hero, who takes the leap. "What's the matter? Scared?"

The tone is familiar to Karl; he knows how to speak this language. "Maybe if you'd take that hat off. For once."

"Oh. So now it's about my hat. A lame excuse if ever I heard one."

"I can't even see your face."

"You're not missing much."

"You're wrong. As usual."

She takes off the Devil Rays cap and faces him, or tries to. Her eyes drop from his to her lap, and then bounce back up, again and again, like a pair of Super Balls.

The next time she speaks, it's without jokes. "I don't think I can stand this much longer, Karl."

Footsteps approach from far away, on gravel. Voices talking: more than one.

Now or never, Karl.

He puts his hand on her shoulder—lightly, in case she swats it away. (She doesn't.) He leans across the gulf . . .

When Jonah and Matt arrive, they find two people under a lamppost, kissing on the bench where Karl said to meet him. So where's Karl?

Unless—no, it can't be—

The kissing couple soon realizes they're not alone. Karl flushes red, Lizette thinks she may die, Jonah doesn't know where to look. Matt says, "Well, well, well, what have we here?"

Karl and Lizette are still fumbling with their Ums and Ers when Blaine, Vijay, and Tim arrive: a head-on collision of Karl's parallel universes.

No massive explosion results, however, because there in the middle of Swivel Brook is a stainless steel turtle shooting out flames, jets of water, and hypnotic music.

"Karl, you're one weird puppy."

"If it's supposed to scare the ducks away, it's not working."

"My grandmother had one of those in her basement."

"I think it's cool. Strange, but cool."

"Flaming Flutes and Fountains! Kooky Creation in Creek! Boy Genius Strikes Again!"

Karl doesn't mind the teasing. In fact, he sort of enjoys it. He has worked on the Turtle for almost a year; his friends' jokes are a warped sort of recognition.

After one last taunt about polluting the public waterways, the gathered teens settle into quiet contemplation. Vijay takes a picture of the Turtle with his cell phone as it plays a dreamy bit of melody. Jonah, smiling serenely, pats Karl on the shoulder.

Stillness falls around them. Lizette, her leg still pressed against Karl's, rubs his ribs with a knuckle and looks left and right, signaling him to check out his audience.

The teasers have turned into gawkers. Mesmerized, they forget to make wisecracks—which is the best response Karl could have wished for.

His world is perfect.

Or, almost perfect. True perfection comes a moment later, when Lizette squeezes his hand and whispers in his ear, "What a guy."

In Case You Were Wondering...

Randall Upchurch withdrew from the mayoral race after the town newspaper published photos of him maniacally clobbering a streetlight with a tennis racquet. The photos, taken by a youngster from a nearby porch, quickly sprouted on computer desktops around town and beyond.

No news of Mr. Klimchock ever reached Abraham Lincoln High School again. A search of his name brought up nothing on Google except an ad for an elderly optometrist in Indianapolis. The handful of students who heard the recording during the SAT assume that he changed his name and moved far away. (They're right.)

The faculty adviser censored Samantha Abrabarba's story about Karl and the SAT. She went on to investigate the finances of the Garden Club (also censored), and unsanitary conditions in the cafeteria—an exposé that she submitted to the *New York Times.* She's still waiting to hear back.

Phillip Upchurch was accepted at Harvard. He plans to join the Parliamentary Debate Society there, attend Harvard Law School, run for Congress, and then—who knows?

· ACKNOWLEDGMENTS ·

MANY THANKS to the teenage students who helped me figure out the facts of high school life and language: Arielle Walter, Sarah Pearlstein-Levy, Louise Webster, and Danny Knitzer. (Note: they didn't tell me anything about cheating. Really!)

Editor Stephanie Lurie proposed the idea for this book to me in five words: "High-tech cheating in high school." I said, "Nah, doesn't sound like my kind of book." Fortunately, when I changed my mind and called her back, she said, "Okay," and went on to offer smart, on-target suggestions at every point. Thanks, too, to: Scott White, supercounselor at Montclair High School, for the basic realities of junior year—transformed here into unrealities. Dr. Elliot Barnathan, for always answering questions that begin "What sort of medical problem could I give a character that would . . . ?" Joe Bleshman, for legal counsel. Mara Daniel, for relaying my German questions to the proper authorities. Steve Albin, for explaining what it means to spoof an address. David Wright, for "the astonishing grace of your lunges." Ira Tyler, for the Czar-dine joke, circa 1970. And, of course, my wife, Jennifer Prost, for answering oddball questions all day long (e.g., "What sort of outfit would a teenager's mother put together for him for a date, using just what's in his closet, if he's not that cool?")—or, let me qualify that: thanks, Jen, for the answers you gave when you didn't say, "How should I know?" Finally, thanks to my tireless research assistant, Google, which answered questions that would have left me stumped ten years ago, usually in 0.003 seconds or less. Thanks, Ya Big Goog.